R.E. Lockett

SILENT ORCHARD RISING STORM

Shadows Beneath the Wings Book 1

WAKELESS RIVER PRESS

Copyright © 2025 by R.E. Lockett

All rights reserved. No part of this publication may be reproduced, distributed, used for training, or transmitted in any form or by any means, including photocopying, recording, or other electronic or mechanical methods, without the prior written permission of the publisher, except in the case of brief quotations embodied in critical reviews and certain other noncommercial uses permitted by copyright law. Be cool.

For permission requests, please write to
Wakeless River Press LLC
3911 Concord Pike # 7674
Wilmington, Delaware, 19803
www.wakelessriverpress.com

This is a work of fiction. The stories, all names, characters, and incidents portrayed in this production are fictitious. No identification with actual persons (living or deceased), places, buildings, birds, beast, fish, plants, and products is intended or should be inferred. In general, don't just go around inferring things.

Published by Wakeless River Press LLC, USA
Made with Human Intelligence.

Not for use in training. Not for AI, not for dogs that love to read, not for dragonslayers, or wizards, or horses, or things that fit outside of that narrow and oddly specific list either. Thank you for your understanding.

Library of Congress Control Number: 2025910474
ISBN:
978-1-955564-09-0 - Paperback
978-1-955564-10-6 - Ebook

1st edition – 2025

For the friends who became family, the places that became home, and the moments that made life an adventure.

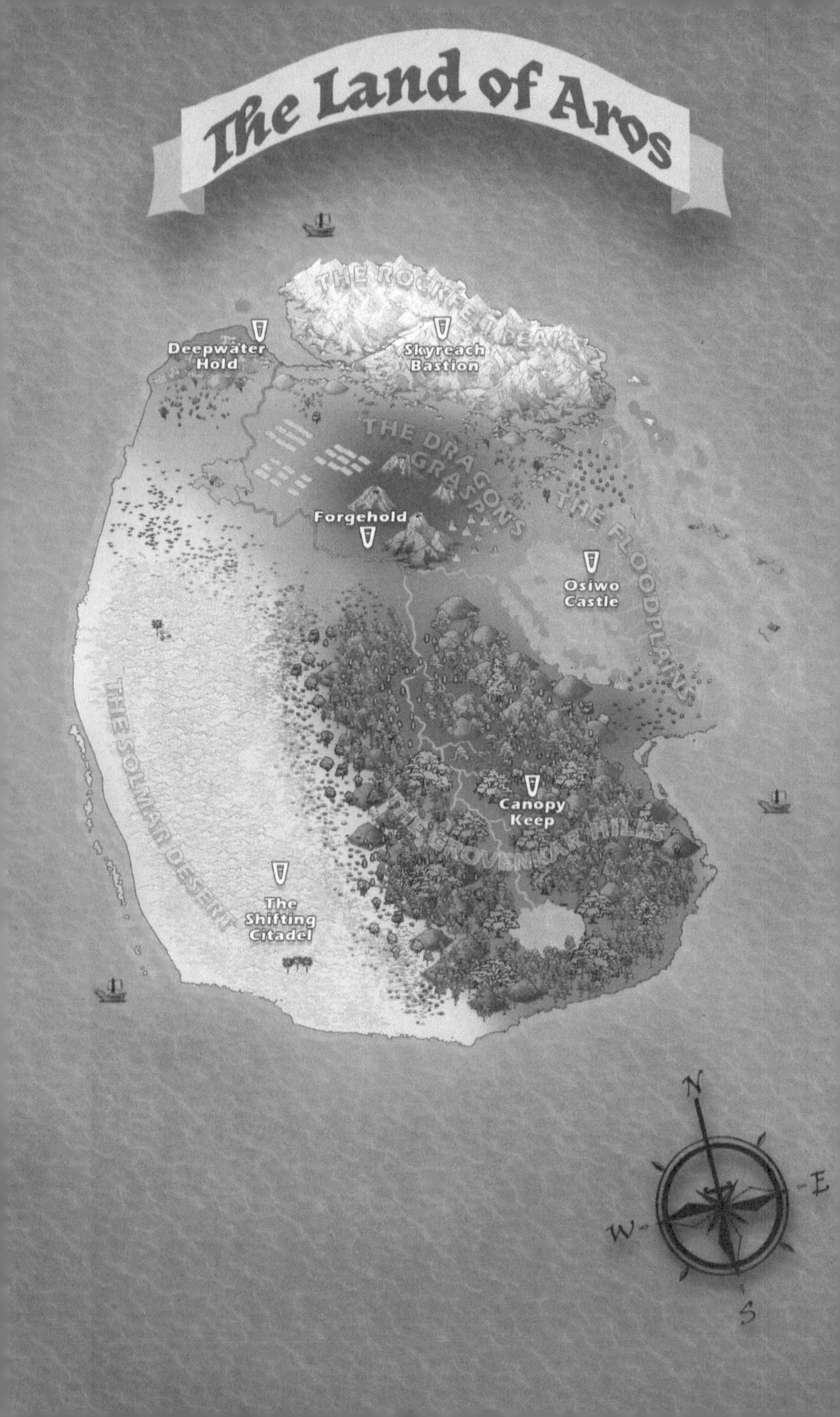
The Land of Aros
Deepwater Hold
Skyreach Bastion
THE DRAGON'S GRASP
Forgehold
THE FLOODPLAINS
Osiwo Castle
Canopy Keep
The Shifting Citadel
N
E
W
S

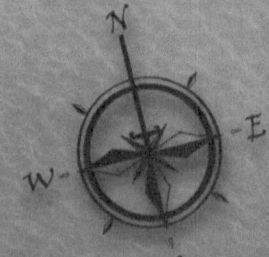

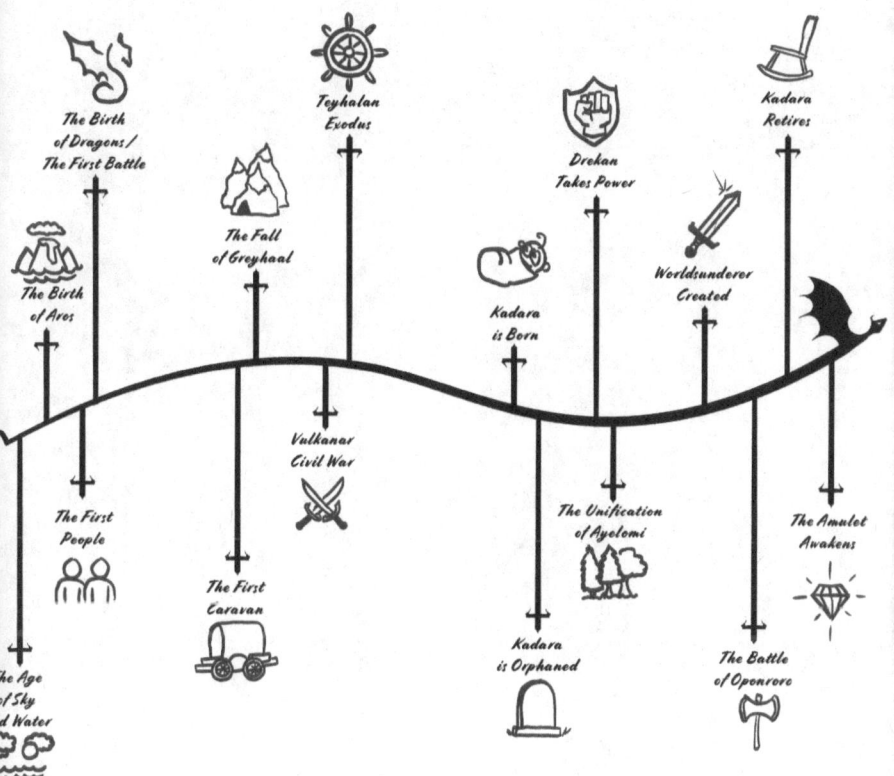

I love you, and I am sorry, and there is more.

Contents

1. A is for Amulet — 1
2. B is for Broken Blade — 9
3. C is for Courage — 31
4. D is for Dragons — 45
5. E is for Everfrost — 61
6. F is for Freedom — 69
7. G is for Greyhaal — 87
8. H is for Heart — 101
9. I is for Island — 109
10. J is for Journey — 131
11. K is for Knowledge — 143
12. L is for Life — 149
13. M is for Movement — 155

14.	N is for Nomad	163
15.	O is for Ojiji	175
16.	P is for Protection	187
17.	Q is for Quarry	193
18.	R is for Recovery	203
19.	S is for Strength	215
20.	T is for Tactics	225
21.	U is for Unseen	233
22.	V is for Vulnerable	241
23.	W is for Waiting	251
24.	X is for Xenolith	259
25.	Y is for Yearning	267
26.	Z is for Zenith	273
Acknowledgements		279
About the author		281

A is for Amulet held near the heart. What once was forgotten now grants a new start.

A SMALL HOLDING EXISTS IN THE NORTHEAST OF NAIWOA WHERE THE FLOODPLAINS GIVE WAY TO RISING SLOPES AND ROLLING MEADOWS. To the far north, tall mountains stretch high into a clinging ring of misty clouds. To the east, the horizon forms a wavering line between sea and sky. Here, the wetlands yield to better drainage, and wildflower blankets cover shallow hillsides. It is a peculiar holding. Most holdings are sectioned by area, and squares are easiest to calculate, so most are square. This one is odd and round. Here, the hills have agreed to roll just once, and all together, creating a gentle mound for a cottage to sit on.

One does. One with a full vegetable and herb garden and a smoking chimney. It overlooks a green grove that runs the full way around the hill and marks the outer boundary of the land. The grove did not exist when Kadara became the owner of the property. That was fifteen years ago. The trees were among the first changes she made. Change is not always good, but it always happens.

A busy market lies northwest of the holding. One can eat two whole apples in the time it takes to travel there if walking. On horseback, more apples would likely be devoured, as horses pulling carts require long, winding roads, and the time to traverse them. A cart-free horse could make the journey in half the time, given that the horse was strong and willing to cooperate. Two apples would be eaten, anyway, if the rider were kind to the horse.

Kadara travels this path often but has never done so on horseback. There was a time when she did most things on horseback, cloaked in full armor. That was before she measured time in apples. That life is long behind her, in the days before she taught herself to weave the long hillside grasses into fruit baskets. Now she stays strong and limber by carrying apples from her grove to the town, stepping like a nimble dancer along an overgrown path that weaves through the hills.

She labors to prepare the market stall each day, joined on three of four sides by other traders. Together they dance a tight choreography of raising poles and tying supports.

When the stall is up and sturdy, Kadara stacks the fruit with care, shining each apple as she places it. Every one is as precious as the next, each a ripe promise of flavor seeming to swell with sweet juices.

The sight of Kadara's apple tower and the sound of her laughter draw customers. She trades the travelers apples for tools and seeds and sometimes even stories. No story is too long to listen to, and if the story is one she will remember, she may offer an extra apple. At the day's end, she breaks down the stall and walks the grassy path home, laden with satisfaction, the goods she traded for, and any apples that remain.

Kadara traveled a vast swath of Aros in her youth, offering her services wherever dragons were doing the greatest harm. Any places she did not visit she was made to study at great length. At the market, she can travel Aros again, if only through her senses. She samples the wine from the Moanaake Islands, reveling in the contrast between its sweet scent and salty taste. The goat cheese brought down from the Rockfell Peaks melts in her fingers on the way to her mouth. Ribbon-like whipfish captured by sailors in the eastern sea swim in glass displays, fed corn and scraps by awed children. A stall farther down the row sells flutes carved from the tube-like skeletons of adolescent whipfish. The owner plays throughout the day, taking song requests from passersby.

In her thick, coiled hair, Kadara wears two short ram's horn braids. They are as black as night but peppered with the stars of age. She is not what she considers old, but age presents itself in different ways for each person. Her eyes are too full of a timeless wisdom to be claimed by a fading youth. She is called "Ms. Kadara" and "Ma'am" by the small children in the town near the market, a town too close to the ever-changing border to be claimed by any kingdom.

The market is on private land, held by a group of merchants who favor prosperity over politics. They are positioned well to accept traders from three kingdoms. Drakhaal to the north, Naiwoa to the south, and Teyhala via the eastern sea all send traders. To trade at the market, a seller must rent a stall. Kadara first rented hers nine years ago, after a long discussion with the merchants to ensure a lack of risk.

Risks are not something Kadara is fond of these days. She has no need for them, nor does she have a genuine need to trade. She owns her private holding and is an excellent gardener. The trees in her grove provide ample fruit. Kadara trades for the joy of being in the market. The hustle and bustle, the noises and smells, they make her heart sing in ways her former life never could.

There were moments in the past, of course, when joy visited her. Now it sits with her most evenings, and they smile together about the new offerings at the market that day. The dragonslayer's life is far behind Kadara, and she never much liked the title anyway.

Though a great deal of respect came with it, she had always tried her best not to kill dragons. In the end, the job was one of endless slaughter. War is insatiable. Each battle feeds the next; each death births a new warrior with a new cause for vengeance, anger, and suffering. So Kadara retired, happy to hang up her sword and cease to be a source of more death in Aros.

She trained in earlier years with one whom some might have called a pacifist, but to her, Orun Jabo had always been a friend. He taught her many things. Foremost were patience, kindness, and the belief that she should "slay for what a thing does, not for what it is." Her mentor had given her all the guidance he could throughout the years and understood her decision to retire. Try as they might, they could not keep her sword unstained, and the weight of the effort pressed like mountains on them both. Jabo had given her his blessing upon her departure, and they went separate ways, forever changed by the work they had done, like hammers made of softer metal than the nails they had driven.

On this morning, Kadara rises with the sun still climbing from the stardust bed it keeps hidden below the horizon. Its rays spy her and insist the sun itself make haste lest she beat them to the well this time. She never notices the sun. A different light breaches her room first.

From an amulet, hanging like a tiny lantern on a thin chain around her neck, a steady blue glow has started. Such a change, yet she finds it familiar somehow, comforting. For her, its luminance is like that of a thousand fires set deep within stone hearths. In its warmth, she feels safe. In its radiance, she feels at home.

Year after year, the amulet has hung from her neck, nothing more than a bauble, a pretty blue stone. It should mean nothing to her, yet she's worn it always and has no other jewelry to speak of. In her memory, she can see herself hanging the amulet from her neck each day. These memories remain fresh, but they have the frayed edges of old knowledge. The amulet has hung on a rope, or twine, or chain throughout the years but always from her neck. Idle, sleeping, waiting.

Now it has awakened, and with it, so has she.

The amulet blooms with a radiance that is soft, not only to the eyes but to the skin. It warms her like midday tea, hearty stews, her favorite chair. She basks in it, letting it wash over her like a new dawn painting a dew-kissed meadow. When she thinks the light will leave, it does not. It stays with her: a new companion.

In the warm blue glow, her every sense becomes sharper, more focused. Sight, smell, touch, taste, and hearing all reach heights she would have thought were reserved for the wilder animals. The azure blanket coats her and chases away the deep shadows in her mind that once hid the path ahead.

She knows this because it has rekindled the fury in two other senses as well: purpose and honor. These are senses she has always had, cohorts of the natural five. Together they kept her younger self honed. Now, she has been sharpened again.

As she breathes in, the blue light seems to follow the crisp morning air into her lungs. She feels it absorb like oxygen into her bloodstream, coursing to her brain. The light cuts away strands like spiderwebs that have enveloped her memories for far too long, and she recalls that the amulet was a gift, one given to her by Jabo upon her departure. How had she forgotten?

A flash of blue streaks through her vision and memories flood her mind like a dry lake bed being filled by a sudden torrential rain.

Ileri stone. It is called an Ileri stone.

Another flash of light, and she sees herself when she first put it around her neck. It was the last time she wore her armor.

The shining steel armor, dulled to gray over the years from disuse, has not been discarded. It rests in a nearby corner where it seems to cower, hiding from its gleaming past in the light of the amulet. This armor was once her only home. Since then, many things have changed. Other things have been left behind. Faces and places have been forgotten, erased when the amulet was entrusted to her. Somehow, climbing into the dull steel shell and bathing in the amulet's light, she remembers them all.

She puts on the rest of the armor, from gauntlet to greaves, marveling at how each piece fits her. It remembers her shape like water, as though someone has re-hammered the metal around her skin. This armor, worn in many battles, was made for many more. The armor was made for her. It was made to protect her, as she was made to protect the world.

And the amulet was made to awaken her, a gift given with intent. All this she knows now but did not remember before today.

Revelation is like armor. It can make one feel less vulnerable, but there is a weight to it. A heavy weight indeed.

B is for Broken Blade, hung on the wall. It's sharper than glass. It will come when she calls.

There once lived a man named Ologun. He was a proud, vain, celebrated maker of weapons. He had earned his pride and vanity, for his was the finest craftsmanship in all of Aros. Warriors, soldiers, scholars, and kings would all come to him for the chance to wield one of his creations. He forged axes and hammers, maces and spears. Knights called themselves by the names of the swords they carried when they carried a sword Ologun had made.

If a weapon could be carried into battle, Ologun could build it. If he knew who was going to carry it, he could improve it. The name Ologun became synonymous with fine weaponry, and lesser smiths found themselves wanting for work because of it. None could match the quality of his craftsmanship, no matter how hard they tried.

One day, a wizard came to Ologun. They sat by his forge and conversed for the whole of three days and more. When the wizard left, Ologun shut the doors to his shop and stoked the fire in his forge. By day, he could be seen working at his wooden bench, curled over some new work of art like the leaf of a drowning plant. Forge light flickered in his window throughout the night. He hid in his workshop and turned away all who came calling. He was working, he said, on his greatest masterpiece.

Days turned into weeks, and the lesser smiths enjoyed the increased work while calling him mad to any who would listen. Business soared without the forge of Ologun to vie with. Battles would always rage on, and inferior weapons needed replacing and repairing often. Without the master forger to maintain them, even the famed weapons of Ologun were growing dull, chipped, and dented.

Rulers sent for the craftsman, offering riches and land, but Ologun had amassed both in his days as an armorer. Hedge knights pleaded with him to help them make their names, earn their land, survive. The sound of his hammer drowned out their pleas. Mercenaries threatened to destroy his workshop if he didn't produce weapons for them, but Ologun was skilled at wielding the weapons he created. He tore through their lower-quality steel like linen and sent them on their way.

After a while, no one came. All alone in his shop on the hill sat Ologun, hard at work while the world moved on without him. He worked and worked on his masterpiece until it reached perfection. When he was ready, he sent messengers to all six corners of the land with three words to share:

OLOGUN HAS FINISHED.

Ologun had not been forgotten. The world's thirst for battle had not waned in his absence, and without a good swordsmith, Death was always the victor, enjoying all the spoils. From far and wide came any in need of a weapon. The lesser smiths came to see their competition. So, too, came scholars and bards. History, according to Ologun, would need a record of this day. He had not only made a sword, he had crafted the finest weapon ever created.

Ologun did not disappoint. For the waiting audience, paid jesters carried a parade of his former weapons through the waiting crowd to a platform in front of the cottage. Bearers of pikes and hammers and flails danced about on a makeshift stage. Some of his former customers joined in, flashing the steel of Ologun-made weapons with pride, smiles of equal brightness beaming on their faces. Food and wine were served on an endless river of platters.

When the six rulers from the six corners of Aros arrived, Ologun invited their retinues to perform fitting entrances. As they entered, Ologun took each ruler's weapon and quickly tended to it, giving it the care it had been missing while he was hard at work. A show of respect and an apology all at once. The rulers received the gesture well. Ologun had planned the entire day with the utmost care, shaping it like he shaped hot steel on his anvil.

When the time came, he lulled the roar of the crowd to a sea of whispers and called attention to the stage, where an assistant brought him a wooden box. Ologun waited for the suspense to build, then opened his box to reveal his great weapon. At first, no one was certain what to think of it. A simple, somewhat small sword sat before them.

The hilt was of a plain design with no embellishments. The blade had neither fuller nor inlay and had only one sharpened edge to speak of. A simple cross-guard offered a gentle upward curve that complemented the bare modesty of the unpolished round pommel. A darkened hide was wrapped around an ebony shell that encased the tang.

Many of the warriors present compared the sword to the weapons they held. Where was the art? Where was the glory? What ornamentation would the bards sing of? How could *this* sword make its wielder a name? Ologun had expected their skepticism, but the sword needed no adornments, no filigree, no jewels. This sword needed no sharpening. It could cut through anything in the entire world, he said. He was so certain that he challenged any wielder to find something his sword could not cut. Should someone find such a thing, he announced, the sword would belong to them.

The crowd did nothing but laugh. Smiths who were present mocked him. The rulers grew angry that their time had been wasted. One young ruler, with an Ologun hammer in his grasp, took the matter into his own hands.

He stood, silencing the rowdy crowd, and crossed the stage in large, powerful strides. When he reached the sword, he brought down his hammer with all his might across the edge of the blade. The ornate head of his hammer slid down the sword, separating into two pieces as it fell. Ologun's sword remained unmarred. The crowd's skepticism was shattered.

Word traveled fast. From every hilltop rang the song of Ologun. Ferries on every river drifted along to the sound of the tale. Of every five souls who heard of the challenge, one was certain to take it. Dark black stones mined from the throat of the Sleeping Mountain came in horse-drawn carts of increasing size and weight. The sword split each stone. Each cart turned back empty (much to the relief of the horses), each challenger defeated. Still more came. Challengers of all statures and strengths came from distances large and small, bearing the hardest materials in Aros.

Diamond and quartzite, glowing ores and petrified woods, contenders brought them all to Ologun's door. The sword cut through each with ease.

Four years passed, and the stream of would-be sword-bearers dwindled to a trickle. Soon, the challengers stopped coming altogether. Ologun was once more alone with his creation.

The sword-maker's property was littered with an assortment of the hardest materials in the world. With his sword, he shaped those hard things, big and small, into a frozen menagerie surrounding his hilltop home. Ologun carved the multitude of stones into every animal he could imagine, from foxes and geese to oxen and lions. When he had no more stones to shape, he fashioned a stand for the sword and set it on his workbench. There, encircled by the hardest of guards, he waited for a staunch champion. None, though, would be worthy of the mightiest sword. None but Kadara.

***

She came on foot. That was what impressed him most. While other challengers had arrived on horseback or by carriage, she seemed to have neither the means nor the wish to make a grand entrance. The others had come for vanity, or glory, and rode in boasting more of the same. Yet, the cloudless dawn, offering a soft, orange sun, reflected against her armor where it could and highlighted dents and scuffs where it could not. This hedge knight came for a weapon while wearing none at her side.

Whereas others might have bandied about, marveling at the garden of sword-sculpted animals, the hedge knight ignored the carvings, intent on her mission. She was still young, though her lack of experience was well hidden by the confidence with which she spoke.

"As a condition for training me, my mentor has sent me to be 'sharpened by the world's greatest blacksmith.'"

Ologun had known many young knights in his day and could see right through the camouflage of her confidence. He did not reply. The cool morning air seemed to revel in the silence.

"I take it you are the blacksmith, and *that* will do the sharpening." Without breaking her eye contact with Ologun, the hedge knight pointed to the sword, waited for the maker's nod, and went to inspect it.

She started by circling the weapon, but rather than seeming to search for filigrees glinting in the sun, she studied the straightness and thinness of the blade. When she did carry it into the light, it was to study the edge on the shadow it made. She grasped the hilt and tested the sword's balance. She tossed it from hand to hand to measure its weight.

"It's as though you've always held that sword," Ologun noted aloud, his interest overcoming his false stoicism.

She ignored him, focusing on her tests.

"A dull axe can split wood with enough force. What about something gentle?" A blade of grass that she snatched from the ground split in two when she laid it on the sword's edge. "Butcher knives can sever sinew, but what of something thinner?" A strand of her hair she laid lengthwise. It, too, split with ease. The hedge knight smiled but did not seem satisfied.

While most had come to Ologun with items intended to dull his blade, the hedge knight brought only a sharp mind and the need for a sword to match it. She gestured toward the workshop. Ologun stepped aside. No others had thought of checking his shop before. Why would they? This inquisitive knight looked for something—perhaps duplicate swords or magic whetstones—but found only a tidy workshop and an irritated smith.

"Have you come to test my blade," he wondered aloud with a grumble, "or my patience?"

Again, she ignored him.

Seeming almost satisfied with the quality—and sincerity—of the sword, she drew close to it. Half-crouched and balanced on her toes, her shadow over the blade, she resembled an alado tree in a mighty wind. Ologun drew in his breath, afraid that this strange new challenger might teeter onto the blade with the slightest gust of air and be split right down the middle.

The knight gathered a deep breath of air as well. Hers, though, she released in a fine stream upon the blade's edge. Its warmth turned into a visible current, tunneling through the crisp dawn atmosphere. Her breath was not simply divided by the sword. Instead, it split like the Apori River, becoming two distinct rivulets that spilled over the edge of the sword. Her smile returned, wider than before, but it did not last.

A shadow stretched over her from a cloudless sky. A dragon had arrived, probably attracted by what it thought was a lazy pack of animals standing unprotected on the hillside. Its mottled blue scales had kept it hidden in the sky until it crossed the sun: a random gift from birth that had no doubt kept it well-fed.

"Get inside," Ologun yelled, but it was too late. The dragon was already diving, and when it saw the glint of the hedge knight's steel armor, it would switch from feeding to fighting without fail.

The knight was too far from the door. She looked from the sky to the sword and back again. Ologun stopped beckoning to her and felt his expression turn to horror as he saw her intention form. "Fool," he said and moved deeper into the cottage to find his bow.

The dragon screeched. It had seen her. As Ologun ran back to the door, he saw the knight grab the sword and take off in a sprint away from the cottage.

A stream of searing, blue dragonfire followed her as she went, the dragon trying to end her with haste.

Careful to keep the blade turned from her, she slid beneath the belly of a bear made of inky black stone. The dragon pounced, slashing at the bear with its enormous claws. The stone was too hard; the dragon could not breach it. The creature rose like triumphant voices and twisted through the sky, searching for a way in while launching a barrage of fire.

The sculpted bear might have kept her from the dragon's claws, but it surely did nothing to block the heat. The knight darted out, ducking and sliding between carved animals. The dragon did not seem amused. Screeching louder, it redoubled its efforts, creating a wall of fire around Ologun's hill.

From inside the cottage, Ologun fired arrows at the dragon, preventing it from hovering long enough to get a fix on the knight. The dragon did its best to ignore him, dodging the arrows and diving at the knight instead. Arrows would not pierce its hide, and the cottage and man within it could be dealt with later.

The knight was visibly growing tired from her constant defensive dashing, and the heat must have made her armor feel like a blacksmith's forge. She flashed the sword at the dragon, enraging it further, and pushed herself into one final sprint. The dragon followed, diving and spitting flames all the way. The knight ran nearly the full circuit of sculptures before spotting the bear again. This time she slid under it feet first, the sword facing up and held with both hands, and cut a deep line into the belly of the bear.

The dragon took the bait. It landed hard on the black stone bear, trying to crush it. As it drew in air to stoke the fire in its belly, the knight drove the sword forward as hard as she could. The tip of the sword, poking up from the bear's back, sliced into the dragon's hide. The beast howled and rolled with the force of an angry tide, sending the bear, the knight, and the base of the sword toppling down the hill. With the sword's tip still lodged in its scales, the dragon howled again and retreated into the camouflaging sky.

When the knight regained consciousness, she was still gripping the sword's hilt. Ologun was splashing water about the hillside, cooling embers, and cursing the dragon. He watched the sky while he worked. The bear had spared the hedge knight the brunt of the fall, clearing the way down the hill like an avalanche. The blade of the sword was still lodged in the sculpted animal, and the knight could not free it despite her greatest efforts.

"Well," the swordsmith said, chuckling as the knight climbed to her feet, "that blade has cut everything from diamonds to dragon scales. There is nothing it cannot cut. If you can name something, the sword will belong to you." He waved his hand in a dismissive nature, accustomed to challengers' failure.

The strange warrior pointed at the sword lodged in the great rock bear.

"It cannot cut itself." She took the bucket from the blacksmith and rinsed her hair and armor with the water that remained.

Ologun took the bucket back from her.

"It cannot." He looked again at the sky and motioned to the humble cottage where he lived. "You are correct. Please, we should talk inside."

***

Steps from the cottage door, Kadara paused to look at the blacksmith. He was holding both the empty bucket and the broken sword, having somehow freed it from the bear. He smiled a reassuring smile and headed inside. She followed him into the cottage and waited while he dragged a chair from in the workshop. It was a cozy seat from beside the forge that seemed to hold the warmth it must've been exposed to over the many years that Ologun had lived and worked there.

"A wizard once sat in that seat. It has been warm ever since. Completely ruined." He winked at his guest, and she pretended to ignore him again, feeling a smile forcing its way to the surface.

Ologun filled a pot and hung it over the crackling fire in the tiny hearth as Kadara looked around at the cottage. It was smaller than she had expected. Her focus had been on the sword when she entered earlier in the day. There on the warm seat, she took in her surroundings and found them to be humble for a world-famous artisan. Further, it seemed the greatest weapon forger in history might be an almost-warm person.

Ornate weaponry decorated the walls, but the art had no doubt been made by Ologun and not purchased for display like that in castle galleries. These weapons were loved and used. The smell of metal oil lingered in the air. The weapons were also cared for. Kadara let her gaze drift farther.

The floor was a simple gray stone that made no attempt to match the darker grays of the stone walls. Aged furniture dotted the interior, ancient but showing little sign of use. The windows had collected more dust than the workbench.

Yet, this was no simple cottage. This was where Ologun had started his meteoric rise. The place where he had made his name.

To think, the greatest blacksmith who had ever lived had only ever lived in one place. Kadara marveled at the idea of permanence. To have a real home—one that was more than the shady trees and occasional inn of Kadara's experience—seemed so far out of reach. Still, with her new sword, she would have a good start.

When the water in the pot was rolling, Ologun removed it from the heat and added herbs, likely from the small garden Kadara had spied outside. She watched him weigh the herbs in his palm and check the temperature of the water. When he saw her watching, he started again.

"I will explain the steps so you can repeat them for yourself in the future."

This time, her smile was irrepressible. She had learned many things, but something so simple as tea had been missed. It felt important in that moment, and she watched with a keener eye.

When Ologun at last handed her a small stone cup filled with the dark, fragrant beverage, she felt overwhelmed.

"Thank you," Kadara said, sipping her tea, "not only for the drink but for the company."

"I, too, am grateful for the conversation. I've had only my animals to talk to for quite some time." Ologun gulped his tea and carried it with the sword to his bench, where he set to work, making the necessary adjustments for the knight who would carry it.

Kadara watched as he removed a handful of small, sunrise-colored shards of stone from his apron. He closed the stones within his fist, kissed it, and tossed the shards into the empty teapot with a yawn. Back over the fire went the teapot. Back to work went Ologun.

The sword's tip had broken off in jagged peaks. He grunted and looked the rest of the blade over.

"I can't repair the blade. It's a special material, you see? It's one of a kind." He turned the blade in the dimming sunlight. It gleamed without hesitation. "I can fuse a new tip on, but it may weaken the rest of the blade." He raised an eyebrow in her direction.

"Thank you, no. It is as it should be." Kadara rose, peered into the pot, and looked across to the workbench, feeling puzzled. "The metal?"

"It isn't metal. Like this grip I intend to forge for you, the blade is made of stone. Dragonstone. It will take several days to become pliable." With a start, Kadara looked over the blade again. To the naked eye, it appeared to be nothing more than steel. The more she looked, though, the more it seemed to shine from an inner source rather than by reflecting the surrounding light.

"Dragonstone? But how?" When she looked back at the smith, he had fallen fast asleep in the warm seat, his empty mug cradled in his hands. She carried him to the soft bed and took his place in the seat, giving in to the urge to sleep herself. So it went, for four days, Ologun trailing off during a story and Kadara carrying him to bed.

"I am dying," he told her on the second day, "but thanks to you, it will be a happy death. I feared I would never find the sword's owner. That it would be buried with me when I went or taken by someone unworthy. I am glad to have met you, Kadara."

"I am glad to have met you, too, Ologun."

Each morning, he would wake as she sat by the fire, watching the dragonstone shards melt down. Each evening, she would make certain he was comfortable and tend to the flames. Though he still grew weaker every day, it seemed her presence was somehow extending the fire in him.

On the fifth day, Kadara was looking down into the red-hot pot when she heard Ologun wake.

She lifted the pot from the fire and turned a smile toward her new friend.

"I have sold countless weapons," he said as she carried the pot toward him. "I have held court for queens and kings. I amassed a fortune during my time as a blacksmith. The shard of dragonstone that I used to make your blade cost me all of it." He shrugged, taking the pot of molten rock from her and setting it beside the sword on the workbench. "Worth every bit, if you ask me. I could always fire up my forge again, but I could never make a weapon so perfect in a dozen more lifetimes. Besides, this life is coming to an end. Every strike of my hammer has led to this moment. By this sword, I am completed." With tongs and special care, he held the blade of the strange sword and dipped the handle into the melted dragonstone, smiling with satisfaction.

Kadara was smiling as well. She knew of dragonstone, though only as a myth. A tale told to inspire children's dreams at night. She had heard it herself as a child, her mind dancing with visions of glory for days afterward. In the myth, dragonstone, the petrified shell of an unhatched dragon, is a fusion of gold, metals, and jewels. A mother dragon eats her treasures when pregnant to soothe the churning inferno in her belly. The hatchlings then devour their shells as a first source of nourishment.

As the tale goes, should an egg not be fertilized in the womb, it does not hatch when laid and becomes a part of the other hatchlings' first meals. Another treasure to devour to prepare for the eventual push from the nest. Would-be dragon hunters held any unhatched, uneaten eggs as the ultimate prize. Ologun had seen them as he saw every other material in the world: as an opportunity.

"It is a loyal material, dragonstone," Ologun explained. "It will always find itself. As long as I had part of it, the rest would always come."

Kadara understood. It must have been how he'd freed the sword from the bear with such ease: the dragonstone shards in his apron.

"It won't hurt itself either. A sword will not cut itself, clever knight, and dragonstone will not either." He pulled the sword hilt from the pot. The cooling dragonstone held to it like river clay. "We must mold it to your grip and join it with you at once."

Before Kadara could react, the blacksmith cut her hand with the sword and thrust the hot, pliable grip into it. She screamed in pain, flailing the hand holding the sword in an effort to release it. Ologun dove for cover, calling out for her to calm herself. Only when the searing weapon sailed from her grasp did she settle, staring at the cut on her hand through tears and confusion.

With blurred vision, she watched as the wound on her hand closed, leaving a thin, golden scar where the cut had been. Ologun sat chuckling in the corner, the sword lodged a wrist's width above his head. He crawled out carefully from beneath the sword and inspected the scar. Seeing whatever it was he'd hoped to see, he pointed to the sword. "Call it."

"But my hand—"

"Is now part of the sword." He turned her palm upward and stepped to the side. "Call it."

The pain in Kadara's palm had faded as quickly as the scar had appeared. It was as though the shining metallic line in her hand had simply been painted on. Only, it seemed to tug slightly toward the sword.

"Sword," she said, but nothing happened. "Come." Still no result.

"Dragonstones don't speak," Ologun offered.

Kadara nodded and looked toward the sword. It did not move, though she'd raised her hand slightly toward it.

"It will take some time. You are still thinking of the sword as an object. It is more than that now. Let us take a walk while you think on it."

The pair marked a long, meandering path around the holding.

"You seem stronger than when I arrived," Kadara said.

Ologun nodded and pointed to his cottage.

"It is one thing to have purpose," he said. "It is another to see that purpose fulfilled. Each is like lightning. When they strike you, you are filled with a primal energy. Your arrival has been a storm of fulfillment, Kadara."

As they walked and talked, Kadara felt the sword calling to her, pulling at her. She found that she knew where it was, like birds know north. It was her true north, now, her magnetic compass. No star would ever shine brighter. When she slept that night, she slept facing the sword. When she woke, it was in her hand.

***

Ologun awakened to the sound of Kadara throwing the sword into his wall and retrieving it. Before he could complain, she flicked her wrist and he watched as the sword slid from the wall without a sound and flew to join her. It settled in her hand as if placed there, and her face lit up with warmth, as if she'd been reunited with a lost love.

"Masterpiece." Ologun sank into the warm forge seat and closed his eyes.

With tea in hand, his noisy guest woke him again. This time, it was to thank him. The afternoon had passed as he slept, the darkness in the cottage growing heavier.

"You are right," she said. "What you have made is not an object, not even a sword. You have forged a tiny, fragile puzzle piece, and it perfectly fills the emptiness I have carried all my life. It is a part of me."

"A masterpiece," Ologun said again. They were his last words. As he died, a blissful grin spread over his face.

Kadara sat with him while the fire in the hearth dimmed, and the night encroached. In the morning, she dug a grave for him where the bear had once stood. She carved a gravestone from the black stone behemoth and dragged it up the hill to mark the place where she laid to rest "THE MASTER OF THE FORGE, CREATOR OF THE WORLDSUNDERER."

Inside the cottage, beside the jar of tea herbs, she found a note addressed to "The Sword-Bearer" that named her the bearer of the humble cottage's deed as well. Ologun had given her more than a start. He had given her a place to finish too. Ologun the blacksmith had forged her a future, but more than that, he had given her a home.

C is for Courage, Conviction, and Creed. For glory, they battle, for honor, they bleed.

THERE ARE LEVELS TO THE AMULET'S GLOW, ITS INTENSITY INCREASING WHEN KADARA IS FACING A CERTAIN DIRECTION. She spins once more to verify. West. The glow is strongest when facing west. When beginning a quest, a direction is helpful. Directions are always better.

With only a notion that she should follow the light, Kadara the Unsworn pulls her sword to her hand and leaves her hilltop cottage, hoping to return. She stops at the inner rim of the grove that surrounds her home, where carved animals peek through the trees, and brushes leaves from Ologun's grave. "Give me strength, Ologun. I know not the path ahead, but I know I should fear it." A breeze pushes through the leaves of the apple grove. "Keep our chair warm."

With that, she sets off through the trees, heading west and into certain danger. She walks along at a steady pace, the flat of her sword resting on her shoulder. She learned long ago that the blade would do her no harm, but no armor is safe from it. Because no sheath or scabbard can hold the sword, she settles for carrying it and planting it in the ground like a flagpole when it comes time to rest.

Her thoughts swim with memories of a version of herself that she no longer recognizes. Gray flecks dapple her hair like sunlight through apple-laden branches, and her skin shows signs of age where it once shone with the radiance of youth. In her memories, she is still fearless, prone to acts of valor, certain of her invincibility.

A lifetime has passed since those days. One filled with peace and calm. Her time is now spent listening to the rustle of the wind through the leaves, tending to her garden and Ologun's grave, and predicting the weather. Adventures are an important part of her diet no more. She has a belly full of salted apples and a head filled with memories that quicken her heart. Still, this task is hers. The light has shown her that.

The high morning sun pulls her shadow westward, like Otun Lake beckoning the waters of the Sunnaford River. She will follow, for now is the time for chasing ghosts and shadows. Reaching the edge of her small holding, she steps from the trees like a winter bear, tired but keen of sense, and follows the west-bound road.

To know the history of Aros is to know the songs of war. They are sung at each battle, and every great battle gives birth to a new song to be sung by all who charge toward the call of glory. The six kingdoms have long been six, varying in size and shape over the years. Populations and landmasses wax and wane with the tides of war and time. Always, though, the rulers hold their castles. Always, they fight and die for more.

The land itself is littered with battlefields and encampments. The dead are burned to make room for more battles. New warriors are born every day. Not everyone fights, though. The laws allow for a somewhat peaceful life. Private land can be neither seized nor confiscated from the holder of the deed. The deed to Kadara's holding, now hidden beneath the stone floor Ologun laid in his youth, notes it as private.

Though this protects the holding from acquisition during a land grab or battle, Kadara has had to defend it from bandits in the past. She would do so again with the joy of a thousand embraces. On her land, her word is law. Once she leaves her holding, the laws of the kingdoms apply.

It has been a lifetime since she traveled the six kingdoms. Certain rules are universal, though. Timeless, like the words of a weathered sign, hung from a post in the recesses of her mind long ago:

Kill outside of battle only in self-defense.

Infraction means death.

A sworn knight may cross borders only with permission.

Desertion means death.

A hedge knight must complete a signed contract.

Nonfulfillment means death.

A ruler's word is law in all their kingdom.

Transgression means death.

When the day fades and the sun finds cause to lay its head on the horizon, Kadara leaves the road and starts a fire beneath a large, wide-canopied tree. A distant tower reaches high into the southern sky, which darkens as she checks the amulet for any directional changes she should make. With west still offering the strongest glow, she scouts the perimeter of her camp.

Fragrant figs and a source of fresh water mix with the scents and sounds of the surrounding wild. A faint hum that she has been hearing throughout the day increases in volume, and she realizes she has been listening to the roar of a battle some miles away. Concentrating, she focuses her newfound, amulet-fed senses and takes in the smell and heat of the clash. It is close. She could reach the battle tomorrow if she had a boat.

She gathers dry wood, figs, and water, and returns to the fading fire. Stoking the flames makes her think of home and the endless warmth of her favorite seat. She boils the water and pulls it from the fire once rolling, as she once saw Ologun do, and as she has done every day since. From a small pouch, she sprinkles dried herbs grown in her hilltop garden.

The tea warms her against the night air, and she watches the fire dance. She cannot remember why she received the amulet, only that it was given to her by Jabo. She presses against the curtain in her mind and sees darkness where answers should be. After a small meal of roasted figs, she decides to rest. With her back against the tree, she tucks away her amulet to shield its blue light and tries to fall asleep.

Sleep never comes, but strangers do. With her senses at their peak, Kadara finds it difficult not to taste the scents on the cool air and listen to the sounds of the night. She tracks a group of armored footfalls traveling the road along the path she took. Her fire is broadcasting her location, so she is not surprised when the travelers leave the road and head toward her. Their abrupt turn allows her to distinguish the footfalls as four different cadences.

She samples the night air. The stink of sweat, weapon oil, and dried fish lingers on the strangers. These are fighting men, well-fed and well-equipped. She is preparing to stand and greet them when she hears the slow, deliberate grind of sword leaving sheath. One of the men has drawn and done so with the quietness of a field mouse. Before this morning, Kadara would not have heard the sound over the crackling of the fire.

Its embers flare and spark, sending an undulating orange glow over Kadara's armor. She lowers her head and pretends to sleep as the group nears, her sword plunged into the ground at her shield arm's side. Three stop at the edge of the campsite, but one continues alone.

"Hold, Bata," one of the stopped says.

Bata keeps moving. "Watch and learn, Redwater."

Though he tries to step without a sound, every footfall is like thunder to Kadara's ears. Adrenaline, she realizes, has further enhanced the amulet's effect. She concentrates on the man's breathing as he approaches. It is as clear to her as if he were a lover speaking adorations in her ear. Waiting with the patience of a transforming pupa, she hears his pulse quicken. Still, she waits.

In Aros, there are wars, battles, skirmishes, and duels. There are also clashes, brawls, scuffles, and tussles. The latter grouping is unsanctioned. Kadara has experience in all the known forms of confrontation, and though the memory in her mind is foggy, her muscle memory is very much intact.

When she hears the man's breath catch, she dodges her head to the left. His lunge drives his sword deep into the tree above her right shoulder. She flicks her wrist, and her sword crosses into her waiting hand, removing her attacker's as it does. She is on her feet before her eyes open. Two more knights step forward, reaching for their swords.

"Hold!" This time, the order takes root. "*Can you not see her quickness?*" the lead knight asks under his breath. "*She is like a sea dragon. Show your steel, and she will devour you.*"

Kadara can hear him with the same ease as she can hear the fool named Bata screaming. She can hear the rapid heartbeats of the obedient knights. She can hear that the lead knight's beats faster.

"Choke off the arm and be silent, Bata," he says.

The knight looks at her sword, her armor, her eyes. "I am Admiral-Knight Rodahn, and you are trespassing on Naiwoan royal land." His eyes drift back to her sword. "Leave that with his and come with us, by order of Queen Senari of the Riverborn." Drawing his sword, he thrusts it into the fire. "Hope that she shows you mercy."

He looks at his more sensible knights and motions toward Bata. "Hold him." Rodahn frees his heated sword from the fire and sets Bata to screaming anew cauterizing the mangled wrist.

While they work on Bata, Kadara reviews her captors. *Senari*, she ruminates, means "wave" in Naiwoan. She had met a Naiwoan princess named Senni long ago. All four knights wear the wave-etched armor and river stone of the Naiwoa. The one who speaks with authority, though, also wears a spiral shell beside the stone that hangs from his neck.

He is Twice-Sworn. No doubt given to the Naiwoan leader as a sign of trust by the kingdom of Teyhala after some skirmish or another. Both are water people, but the Naiwoans vie for power while the Teyhalans wish only to sail the seas. Kadara wonders about the man's allegiance. Does his heart call for the sea, or is he here because of his thirst for battle?

She spins, perhaps with too much verve, and drives her sword into the bark of the tree. The sound startles everyone except herself and the lead knight, who lets out a hearty laugh. He sheaths his sword and starts back toward the road while the others kick dirt over the fire and push her along behind him.

When they reach the road, they turn north and follow it until they arrive at one of the many waterways that coil like mangrove roots along the floodplains. There, Kadara is made to board a flat, woven, circular boat used by Naiwoan scouts to navigate the waterways' sharp turns. She steadies herself, cataloging the distinct scents in the saturated, blue-streaked clay and decomposing plant matter along the riverbank as the water laps at the sides of her newest means of travel. The direction favors Kadara, as evidenced by the warmth of the amulet hidden behind her breastplate.

The trip to the war camp is long, protracted further by the incessant griping of Bata, who ceases his complaining only to hold his tongue as they pass river dragons on the bank. A healthy fear of dragons sees the water people through to old age. Rodahn and the other two knights, whom Kadara comes to know as Shin and Galago, do their best to drown him out with war songs and questions that Kadara refuses to answer. By the time they reach the encampment, morning has full hold of the world and midday is wrestling for control.

After disembarking, Kadara waits while the knights gain entry. With little effort, she is able to focus her hearing on the camp's entrance. The guards look shocked and amused while Rodahn relays the story of his new prisoner.

"Keep her on a leash," one says to Rodahn as he waves his party forward, "and find one for Bata."

The song of Rodahn's laughter escorts them as the guards swing open the makeshift gates and smirk at Bata as the group passes. Shin and Galago escort Kadara to a cage made of hardened reeds while Rodahn goes to speak to his ruler.

Bata stands nearby, relaying to Kadara all the tortures he will be invited to visit upon her once his queen hears of the insult to one of her sworn knights. As he speaks, Kadara watches the tip of a spear bobbing above the river of knights in the direction that Rodahn went. It stops suddenly, then spins and heads toward them as if caught in a fast, direct current. Kadara can make out only a long stretch of decorated pole below the spearhead moving in her direction. Its owner does not seem concerned with the multitude of knights in their path. They keep a steady, unbroken pace as if expecting the warriors to simply part for them to pass. The warriors do.

They straighten their backs and stand their spears at their sides like statues. When the last two swing aside like an armored door, the queen of Naiwoa steps through, Rodahn and a handful of clerics on her heels.

Her dark hair is long, tied up in intricate braids that resemble flowing rivers. Her eyes are a bright, piercing blue, evoking the clear waters of her homeland. Tattoos of rippling water run along her arms and neck. Her armor, made of lightweight, polished metal and reinforced leather, shimmers like water in the light.

A spear hangs from her back, its spearhead rising like the dawn sun. She steps through the parting knights like a river cutting through the plains and settles onto the scene like pooling water, her retinue spreading around her. Her mere presence silences Bata. Queen Senari of the Riverborn seems to be a woman accustomed to silence. It likely greets her every arrival. Here, it is a silence so deep that she could listen to the river laugh as the sun rises over the sleeping floodplain. Today, however, she is at war. Silence can do her no good here.

"Speak, you damnable fool, or I will take your head and leave the rest of you for the river dragons." She does not look at Bata, her eyes fixed instead on the prisoner whose presence demands her attention. She cocks her head with a look of puzzlement, her gaze still on Kadara, and leans her long, intricate spear toward the silent Bata, coaxing his tongue to work.

"The Unsworn, she—she took my hand." Bata bows to his queen, inching lower with each word, and presents his bandaged wrist as evidence.

Kadara was happy to play along while it met her needs. Now, though, the amulet beneath her armor lies cold, dormant. She needs to find a direction. She needs to keep moving. She speaks.

"Your man drew his blade while approaching." Her words are steady, measured.

"I meant only to defend myself." Bata waves his bloodied arm at the reed cage holding Kadara.

"Against a campfire?" Kadara chuckles and waves him off.

"Enough," the Naiwoan ruler snaps. Her focus never leaves her prisoner. "You have trespassed on my land. Bata was wrong to draw unannounced, but punishment must be given, regardless."

Bata seems pleased with this development. Encouraged enough, even, to risk lifting his eyes. He visibly bathes in the cooling flow of his victory and floats a broken, yellow smile at Kadara. Kadara ignores him, more concerned about finding the path ahead and wondering how long this queen's apparent interest in her will delay that.

The queen's gaze sharpens. Impatience falls back toward puzzlement before turning towards what could be a look of recognition.

Kadara realizes in this moment that recognition will be something that continues to haunt her despite her long years away from the madness across Aros. People will recognize her, or her sword. She will not likely know them, even if she once did. Time changes people, and the amulet took much when it was given to her. She waits for the answer to this mystery, hoping it will soon present a chance at freedom.

"What punishment, then?" Kadara asks. The queen gazes at the gleaming tip of her spear, a look like longing passing over her face.

"Torin Halfhammer is making a grab for my northern stretch, and I am now down by one hand." The queen lets her gaze drift to the prisoner again. "I have mine full enough with Drakhaalan soldiers trampling the banks of Naiwoa. I won't have an Unsworn adding to the trouble. Twenty days for trespassing. It is a lengthy sentence but a fair one. My father wrote it to aid the homeless along the river. Twenty days in Osiwo is enough to convert anyone."

Rodahn bursts with laughter, and the queen glances at him. Senari's smile sinks beneath the surface of her calm demeanor, and she continues in a half-whisper, "I remember you, Dragonslayer. I don't need to see the scar on your palm to recognize you. I remember what you did for my father. I remember what you did for me." Louder, she says, "I will waive the sentence should you contract to me for half that length of time."

"No." Bata is incensed. "She destroyed me, took my hand, my livelihood, and now she is being given back her sword and offered the glory of battle? No, I think not. I will not fight beside this lordless one."

"No. You won't." Kadara sinks into the shadows and sits at the rear of her cage. The queen nods and turns to other matters, parting the knights as she goes. Bata swims in his triumph, goading Kadara.

"Age has sapped this one's will to fight, Redwater. Maybe her wits as well."

"Silence, fool." Rodahn strikes him like an oar hitting water. For one with such a keen sense of humor, he appears just as expressive in his lack of amusement. "You drew your sword on an unarmed knight and disobeyed a direct order from your superior. You'll be sharing the cell next to this one unless you bleed out in the night."

He motions to Shin and Galago, who force Bata into a nearby cage and follow their leader through the crowd toward the front. As they do, the amulet flushes warmth against Kadara's armor. The path has been made clear again.

In twenty days' time, Kadara will be back on the road, back to finding answers, back to fulfilling her task.

The warmth fades.

Kadara reminds herself to be patient.

The warmth returns.

She considers the benefit of having her sword in hand, of being on her way ten days sooner.

The warmth fades and returns and fades again: a slow, unsteady heartbeat. Something is circling her. When the heat returns, it sears. The glow of the amulet paints her chin in a river clay blue, and she winces in pain. Before she can fish the amulet from her armor, Bata screams his loudest scream yet.

D is for Dragons in sea and in sky, with flames in their bellies and gold in their eyes.

As long as songs have rung from Aros, they have been the songs of battle, and the songs of battle quicken the hearts of none more than the dragons. At the Dawn of Aros, while the people were still in their infancy, they wandered a dragon-less world seeking knowledge. Enlightenment and comprehension eventually gave way to envy and coveting, and soon after came violence. When the First Battle roared, the crust of the Mother's Valley lurched and split. It spat forth the four volcanoes that make up the Dragon's Grasp: the Sleeping Mountain and the Three Claws.

As they rose, the volcanoes pulled the earth with them. A tremendous upheaval, it caused the Apori River to split into the Sunnaford and Te-Orani Rivers that run west and east from the base of the mountain.

The battle raged on. The Three Claws erupted.

The steam from the river washed over the battle as a thick, hot cloud, the Sleeping Mountain rising above it. As the battle reached its peak, the Sleeping Mountain spewed forth Inati N'tan, the first dragon. The Terror of the Skies was thrown roaring into Aros and soared into a murderous frenzy.

Dragons have appeared in the skies over every great battle since, spitting fire and consuming combatants. Some call the clanging of swords "the dinner bell," and no battle is deemed glorious without a dragon.

When the fighting of the First Battle stopped, it had been going on for days, and Inati N'tan had devoured half of all the warriors in the world.

Those who remained fled to the six corners of Aros to heal, train, and prepare for the next battle.

So it was that men like Bata, who had never seen a glorious battle, would never have come face to face with almost certain death at the fangs of an angry dragon. When a warrior has been close enough to a dragon to smell its sulfur breath and feel the heat emanating from its furnace belly, they know that screaming will do them no good. Kadara had charged at the enormous, fanged jaws of many dragons. Only her cunning and her sword helped her to survive. She had always let others do the screaming.

Kadara was once young, and Senari—Senni—was once younger. Years ago, when Senni was a willful princess and her father had ruled this land, Kadara took her first contract as a dragon hunter from King Jor of the Floodplains, ruler of Naiwoa. She was skilled but untrained, wearing armor she had found in the cottage left to her by Ologun. Though it fit her well, the polished metal shone too much. The armor was free of damage, free of dirt. And Senni was keen. Her blue eyes pierced the confident shell of Kadara's demeanor.

She pointed out the signs of inexperience to her father and all in the chamber. Kadara was unbothered. She latched on to this truth, asking how much experience the hunters before her had claimed to have. For all the experience that preceded her, she continued, Jor still had a dragon on his lands and the reward purse in his pocket. The exchange made the king bark with laughter. Kadara earned the contract and a room for the night, right there in Castle Osiwo, to rest and prepare for her mission.

The Naiwoan royalty, enjoying an almost mystical connection to the river, the lake, the floodplain, presented Kadara with a feast of freshwater fish and oysters. With this came fresh bread made from floodplain grains and sweet roots—a delicacy from the Moanaake Islands to the east.

When Kadara was ready to sleep, she was escorted to a room that shone with the reflection of the pale blue water beneath it.

Princess Senni was there waiting for her, wooden sword and paper armor at the ready. Kadara indulged the small girl while she showed off her fighting stance, noting that the girl moved like water even at that early age. When she said good night, the princess thanked her for coming to help. Kadara had slept well through the night—one of her last full nights of sleep for some time—and left early for her hunt.

The sun was still peeking over its wave-topped blanket when Kadara reached the dragon's den. It was a seaside cave southeast of Castle Osiwo at the end of a long, rocky beach. Though she had declined the knights Jor offered to assist her, she heard the careful footsteps of the three watchful guards behind her as she approached the dark mouth of the dragon's hideaway.

She paused, letting the incoming wave run over her boots and suck her feet deep into the sand as it rushed back out. Her followers caught up and pressed ahead without her, each hoping to claim the glory that their king was so willing to pay outsiders for. Kadara had taken lives before but only in self-defense. She was in no hurry.

To hunt, stalk, and kill something with no more cause than money was difficult for her to contend with. This dragon had hurt no innocents, to her knowledge; it hadn't scared away the precious bounty of fish that the Naiwoans coveted. This dragon was expected to die because it existed. It had killed countless dragon hunters for the right to continue existing. Now it was considered a menace, cruel and deadly. Had dragon hunters not made it so?

Kadara decided that this dragon, this Dorvan the Cruel, had not earned her sword that day. She turned her face to the rising sun and let its heat warm her skin. By chance, she opened her eyes to see the young princess barreling toward her, intent on entering the open mouth of the cave.

The dragonslayer reached out to grab the girl, but her boots had sunk too deep in the sand by then, and she stumbled as she yanked her feet free, missing the girl's arm by inches. By the time she regained her footing, the girl had vanished, gone deep in the den somewhere to play at being a knight. Kadara cursed her lack of speed and bolted into the den after the girl, calling her name.

Though Kadara had been practicing the silent pull of her sword for some time, sprinting and diving along the path where the blue sky dragon had chased her before Ologun's death, she now wished she had practiced navigating in the dark or making torches instead. The darkness of the cave was as suffocating as its thick, stagnant air.

She pressed on, hoping to hear the girl's footsteps. Instead, she heard screaming. Increasing her haste, she followed. It is not wise to sprint through the darkened dens of dragons. It is less wise still to continue sprinting when the cavern ahead is well lit by dragonfire.

Kadara blinked her eyes, taking in the light and examining the scene. Two of the three Naiwoan knights who had trailed and then rushed before her remained standing. The third had been crushed under the enormous front foot of the scaly red beast. The knights assailed the dragon from either side with long, sharp pikes but could not pierce its hide. Patches of dragonfire dotted the cavern where the flames had taken hold, threatening to join and trap them all inside.

From a passage on the far side of the cavern came Princess Senni, her wooden sword outstretched, her roar like a tiny typhoon. Kadara sprinted in her direction. Dorvan's golden eye flickered to the girl for an instant—and Kadara held her breath—but the dragon had no interest in the small attacker.

Before Kadara could reach Senni, the dragon spun and lashed its tail at her, knocking her back. She rolled, scouring the cavern for Senni. Again, the girl pressed her attack. This time, her wooden sword made contact, glancing off the dragon's scarlet tail. Kadara rose and made another attempt at retrieving the girl, only to be knocked back again as the dragon rounded on the second knight.

Senni charged once more, thrusting the tiny weapon into the dragon's foot. Dorvan spied her again, with lingering eyes this time, and nudged her aside, opting instead to whip his tail at Kadara. She ducked, cursing herself for being distracted, and called for Senni to run.

Dorvan looked about and charged at the first knight again. The knight's armor gleamed as he retreated into the maze of tunnels. The dragon followed. When screams tinted with a shade of hysteria echoed from the tunnels, Kadara's mind hunted for a way to get the princess out alive. The remaining knight charged down the tunnel after the blood-red dragon, her armor gleaming as the other's had. Kadara leaped to her feet. In a whirlwind, she tore off her armor, tossing it onto the sand. Her tunic stuck to her, soaked with sweat from the heat of the cave.

Another scream came from the tunnels, and one of the knights scrambled out, his gaze wild with fear. It fell on Princess Senni, and the knight ran forward and grabbed the girl with a rough grip, yelling at her to get behind him.

Kadara was crossing the cave in long strides when the dragon reappeared, a knight hanging from its maw. It looked at Kadara and chomped down the meal. Without her sword in hand and stripped of her armor, Kadara posed no threat.

The dragon's head rolled to the right, and its eyes fell on the fear-mad armored knight. The knight spun, tossing

Senni to the ground like a dented shield. Dorvan could not see the girl, but Kadara knew she had to act before it was too late. Dorvan reared up, preparing a burst of dragonfire. It never came. Kadara had slid beneath the belly of the dragon, whispering an apology to the oft-harassed beast, and sliced Dorvan's belly open, extinguishing the fire within.

Senni was bruised but alive. She hugged her knees, sobbing, and shoved her paper helmet behind her in shame when she saw Kadara approaching. The knight tried to speak but could only stutter. Kadara struck him hard across the face and picked up the tiny wooden sword that Senni had brought with her. The knight backed away from Kadara, looked at the slain dragon, and turned for the cave exit, never once checking on the princess. When Kadara glanced back in his direction, he was gone, and the shafts of light filtering in from the cave mouth had begun to dim.

The knight was burying them inside the cave. Kadara knelt to be at eye level with the princess and handed her the toy sword. The girl looked smaller than before, clenched like a tiny fist against the dangers of the world. Seeing the certainty in her hero's eyes, she took the sword, then Kadara's hand, and let the dragonslayer lead her to the exit. When they reached the cowardly knight's makeshift barrier, Kadara sliced with her sword through the fallen rocks and rubble. Cool beach air rushed in from beyond.

By the time they arrived at the castle, Senni lay asleep in Kadara's arms. Her armor left behind in the cave, the dragonslayer entered the grand hall cradling the princess and interrupted the feast being held there. The confused look on the king's face suggested the returning knight had left out a good deal of the story. The angry look on the queen's face suggested a large portion of the missing story had been Senni's part in it. The knight's face mirrored the king's confusion. He clearly thought he had left Kadara and Senni to die.

Kadara laid the tiny princess in the arms of a maid-in-waiting and pulled her sword to her from where it waited in the sand beside Dorvan's cave. It came with the calm of a cool breeze. It was never needed. Jor was no fool, and his Ologun-made spear flew straight and true. The dishonest knight was dead before Kadara felt her sword's hilt in her hand. She left Castle Osiwo that day with a chorus of apologies echoing in her ears, twice the agreed-upon purse, and a lingering uncertainty about the morality of dragon slaying.

***

F

rom her hardened reed cage, Kadara has a good view of the battlefield, a place where morality is not being discussed.

The frenzied, blue sky dragon lands with explosive force, face first, mouth open and around Bata's cage. The energy is so powerful that Kadara, inside her cage, is thrown clear. The dragon rears back, flinging chunks of grass and mud from the small crater that had been the ground beneath the cage, and swallows the still-screaming Bata.

A ripple of panic shivers through the battalions on both sides, swelling into a tidal wave of sheer terror as horror and belief fuse into a potent mixture. The dragon pounces, its attack indiscriminate of the armor etchings, trinkets, and banners that identify the Naiwoan and Drakhaalan warriors. It spreads terror with its magnitude alone. Its golden eye, the size of a market stall, drinks in the sight of frenzy like aged wine.

Kadara, from a cage sinking into the mud, reaches out to call her sword, hoping to cut herself free. The dragon appears to respond in the weapon's place, crossing the battlefield toward the trapped dragonslayer and roaring with rage.

Admiral-Knight Rodahn crosses the field as well. In the wake of the dragon's arrival, he continues to fight, focusing more on the dispatching of his enemies than on the glory of the moment.

He pulls weapons from downed enemies and comrades alike, depositing them in any foe foolhardy enough to cross his line of sight. When his gaze falls on Kadara, he sends a Drakhaalan hammer hurtling toward her. The hammer shatters what little remains of the cage as the dragon drives it, and Kadara, deep into the mud.

Kadara does not panic. Flailing and kicking will only draw water from the saturated soil and hasten the sinking. Still, something feels odd—a familiar tug of something nearby. Her senses flare like light through a prism. She can feel the dragon's rattling lungs expelling air, a thousand panicked heartbeats scattered across a broken battlefield, the approaching footfall of Rodahn. She can feel her sword.

If she can retrieve it, she can cut her way free of this quicksand mire. She reaches out again, grasping at anything above the surface, and senses something unexpected: the shard of her sword buried in the dragon's thigh. The creature shrieks in pain and leaps into the air with Kadara still summoning the shard. The force of the dragon's movement lurches her free from the mud. She shoots upward as if propelled by a geyser, mud and dirty water spreading like rumors behind her. Once in the air, she releases her pull on the shard and slams hard into the wet ground beneath her.

The great blue menace drills its stomach against the ground and drags it along, crushing anything in its path. Kadara pulls again, this time harder, and the dragon charges at her, its golden eyes gleaming with hatred, and shrieks of pain pouring from its fanged jaws. It rams its tail back and forth, hammering through anything still standing in its wake. Kadara cannot rise fast enough. A stream of weapons comes to her aid.

Rodahn is sprinting toward her in the dragon's path of destruction, collecting and heaving the weapons of the fallen as he runs. His infectious laughter rings out as he goes. As the dragon whips its tails at the brave knight, a spear whistles through the air and slices through its enormous, leathery wing. Senari will not be denied glory on this day. The dragon bellows in anger and rises into the air, spraying dragonfire as it goes. When it disappears into the northern sky, Kadara turns to thank Rodahn, but he is on the ground and in pain, the tail of the beast having made contact after all.

"Ro!" Senari reaches him first, leaving a long track in the mud as she slides onto her knees beside him. "Ro," she says again, taking his hand. "Ro, you're making me look bad."

Rodahn coughs out a laugh and tries to sit up.

Having retrieved Senari's spear, Kadara approaches, her senses still at their peak. She listens to Rodahn's heartbeat. The strong rhythm tells her he is wounded but not gravely.

The apparent lovers come to the same conclusion, and Senari regains her composure. She calls for transport. "Get him home at once. His healer is the best in Aros."

She takes her spear from Kadara and motions for the hedge knight to follow. Her retinue needs no invitation, and they trail along, listening and passing down orders as needed. "Send word once you arrive in Teyhala and when you are departing to return home," transport is told. "Take a fore scout and a rear and do not stray from the road for any reason. I will lose no further Naiwoans today." She stops, and the injured Rodahn is carried forward on a wagon. Field medics have strapped him down to prevent movement. His sword lies across his lap. Bandages soaked in blood cover his torso, but he smiles as if he were out for a casual ride.

"I might decide to return to you," he says to Senari, smiling.

"Only come if you can fight."

Rodahn coughs up another laugh, much to the irritation of the nurse riding with him, and waves goodbye to the war camp while keeping eyes locked on the only person there who matters to him. Chants of "Redwater" follow him as he goes.

Senari smiles and then sets her expression to the stern, contemplative one of a commander. She spins to face Kadara. "I want that dragon dead."

Kadara glances across the field of dead and dying soldiers to the ruined cage, still visible in the mud.

"I invoke my right as ruler of Castle Osiwo to replace your sentence with a task, Dragonslayer. This is the task I give. Kill that dragon."

"Vengeance?" Kadara's voice is low; her patience is being tested. "Please, I am on a quest. Let me serve my sentence and be on my way."

The queen is not without mercy, and even in her angered state, she is like a tidal river with mangrove banks. The fullness of her rage may ebb and flow, but the foundation of her rational thinking appears undisturbed.

"Where does your quest take you?"

From inside her armor, Kadara pulls out the chain holding her amulet and lets the stone spin in the air between them.

"The light is now strongest when pointing north," Kadara admits with reluctance.

"Then it seems your quest and your duty are intertwined. Go north into Drakhaal, Dragonslayer Kadara. Follow Halfhammer's half-wit horde. They will trample the path through the mountains well enough for you to track. Avoid Torin if you can. He won't be pleased to see the sword that made his name. When you find the blue dragon, take its head. This I command."

As Kadara stows her amulet in her armor, she chuckles and looks into Senari's eyes.

"You have grown to be a fair and frightening ruler, little Senni." She raises her hand high and summons her sword, which comes whirling through the air and into her waiting palm.

"I have grown to be a ruler with funeral pyres to light." Senari lashes her spear to her back and calls for a horse. When it arrives, she hands the reins to Kadara. "Go. Give me fewer pyres to light in the future."

E is for Everfrost, embers of ice. If the burn doesn't kill you, the freeze will suffice.

NORTH IS NEVER JUST NORTH. Not in the mountains. Kadara weaves back and forth up the mountain pass on horseback until the mare slows. When it does, she dismounts and sends it trotting back down the rocky path. Better that it have energy for the journey home than die broken and cold somewhere between the snowy peaks.

The amulet's warm glow tells her she is, then isn't, then is headed in the right direction as she winds along, following the promised, trampled path of the homeward-bound soldiers ahead of her.

She thinks of Castle Osiwo as she walks, wondering how King Jor died and whether he knew his daughter loved a Teyhalan warrior. She can almost hear Jor laughing as she crests another stony outcropping. The laughter echoes about, and Kadara realizes that what she's hearing is not laughter at all.

She sets her sword down and concentrates on the noises. They fade to silence, her presence having clearly been sensed. She is not alone, and she suspects her company is not human.

She is in the mood neither to remove her armor nor to slaughter dozens of rock dragons, so she hesitates, deliberate, ready to pull her sword should the beasts take her for a threat or an easy meal. They have made themselves unseeable, but their sounds do not keep them invisible to Kadara. To her, they have mass and are tense and far too close.

The size of the group of knights who preceded her must have been enough to deter any rock dragon attacks, but Kadara has no such luck. The laughing barks of the dragons turn to excited yelps as they catch sight of her armor. Kadara is patient. The memory of taking a life is a heavy thing. She carries too many such memories as it is. Making another will require an absolute need. She hopes these dragons don't provide one, but a hungry dragon can't survive on hope. In the orchard of life, every apple carries seeds of both hope and sorrow; every moment is ripe with equal potential for joy and pain.

The dragons attack.

Unlike the titanic sea and sky dragons, rock dragons never grow much larger than wildcats. They stalk the high altitudes, shifting their scales against the sun to camouflage themselves in the rocky terrain. They are invisible, goat-hunting menaces, and Kadara has encountered them before. Last time, the dragons had the advantage. This time, though she cannot see them, she can hear their breathing. She can hear, also, the gravel slide beneath their clawed feet, the high mountain winds brush against wings too small for flight. This time, she can kill them all. Yet, this time, like the last, she runs.

Painting a moving, mental picture of the dragon pack pursuing her, she watches for holes in the ice ahead. The pack leaps the voids while launching a barrage of everfrost in her path. As the volleys land, they explode into blue, glowing, tree-like columns of ice, reaching with deadly branches that freeze whatever they touch. Kadara dodges and rolls, keeping her lead all the while, and ascends the mountainside like a leaf rising on an angry wind, the amulet's warmth intensifying as she climbs.

Statues line the path on either side of her. *Sculptures*, she thinks as she passes one. The near-perfect details threaten to distract her, and she turns her head as she passes another. The eyes seem to follow her from behind a murky blue glow. *Soldiers*, her mind corrects. Frozen soldiers. An injured Drakhaalan comes bounding toward her, his arm a frozen stump, broken off at the elbow. His eyes tell her she is going the wrong way. They remain that way, two wide, white, unmoving alarms, as a ball of everfrost flies over Kadara's shoulder and hits him square in the chest. Kadara never stops moving. She spins past the newest victim of the ice, careful not to make contact. She must reach the gates of the stronghold or be frozen herself, cursed to wait for the dragon horde to devour its icy catch.

With her amulet-powered hearing, she paints a picture of the icy trail ahead and calls her sword from the rear. It mows a path up the mountainside and reaches her hand, decimating most of the pursuing pack. Ahead of her, the soldiers are contending with a separate pack with what little remains of their strength. A single soldier sprints farther up the mountain, away from the fighting, probably seeking to bring back help, but it will be too late.

Kadara has a distaste for killing, but she also has a duty not to let people die. As the remains of the dragon pack following her recover, she dives into the fray. The soldiers cheer, happy to see a hedge knight coming to their aid. They would cheer less if they could see the terror she drags along behind her.

Kadara focuses on the spitters first. An armored fighter can bear the physical assault of a rock dragon, but everfrost cannot be parried; it cannot be blocked. She moves with too much speed for the distracted dragons ahead to react. Accustomed to being unseen, they do not shy from her approach. They do not know how to respond to being hunted. The combination of their confusion and the scent of brethren dragon blood sends the remaining rock dragons into a frenzy, much to Kadara's delight. A frenzied dragon, she learned long ago, is one focused only on attack.

When a rock dragon focuses on ripping someone limb from limb, it ceases to focus on shifting its disguising scales, on building bursts of everfrost in its belly. A frenzied rock dragon is vulnerable; it is one that everyone can see.

The Drakhaalan soldiers show no hesitation. These warriors have just seen their kin slaughtered by another attacker, a sky dragon. These fighters have been set upon by a pack of rock dragons while trying to return home with what few ranks of theirs remain. They are desperate people, and Kadara will side with desperate people over frenzied dragons any day.

She moves about, slicing at any charging dragons and deflecting blows meant for the eagle-feathered cloaks billowing at the soldiers' backs. The dragons do not let up, charging in pairs and triples and barking like Jor gone mad. As Kadara begins to tire, she hears the faint thunder of hooves on rocky soil, storming down the hill like an avalanche.

"They come," she says, but no others can hear the drumming of salvation on its approach. She cuts through another dragon and shouts again, pointing toward the gates of Skyreach Bastion, high in the Rockfell Peaks above them. The gleam of armor can be seen descending the slope. The fighters redouble their efforts, charged by the knowledge that they will soon be saved.

Twelve horses arrive, their hooves falling hard on the ice as riders swing hammers from atop their backs. They clear the remaining dragons and create a fearsome perimeter for the wounded to be supported in their journey up the rest of the mountain. When Kadara reaches the gates, she is told to head back down the path. She is tired and not in the mood to argue. As she turns to leave, the war-ravaged soldiers spring to her aid, demanding she be permitted to pass.

"Who are you, hedge knight?" A long-cloaked Drakhaalan knight strides through the crowd, addressing her. "Who are you that these men would risk further injury to secure your passage?" The other soldiers, all of shorter cloak, give him a wide berth.

The feathers of his extravagant cape bristle as she speaks.

"I am no one." She bows her head, avoiding eye contact. "Merely passing through."

The knight's gaze paints her in skepticism, darting from face to sword to feet and back again, tracing her in full for maximum effect.

"We are in the highest mountains in the north-east-most corner of the world, Unsworn. There is no 'passing through.' This in stone."

This in stone. Kadara recognizes the phrase from a Drakhaalan trader she often sees at the market. Like this knight, the trader uses it as a punctuation of certainty. Like this knight, the trader is wary of strangers.

The long-cloaked officer motions for two half-cloaked, bedraggled warriors nearby. "This hero has been granted entrance to Skyreach Bastion," he says. He mounts a horse that he did not arrive on and looks back at her. "In chains."

Kadara does not protest. The steel shackles are heavy and dig into her wrists when she allows her arms to hang, but she does not complain. She could cut through these men like stewed carrots and carve her way through the mountain-settled stronghold while "passing through," but bloodshed never has a purpose. It is fed by desire and fear, and written into history with glory and excuses. Once again, Kadara is imprisoned as she's taken toward her goal. Destiny, she thinks, is a dragon-hearted tyrant.

Her captors take her sword and drag it along, blade down, hoping to dull it. They cannot. Instead, they carve a long, deep line along the path that snow covers behind them. An exhausted smile breaks Kadara's stony demeanor as they near the stronghold. The amulet is warm enough now to beat back the cold.

If destiny would force her up the mountain, it might also free her from its icy grasp. Of all the lessons the wizard Jabo had taught her, patience was the one used most often. It was also the one most tested.

Kadara understands now that the Ileri stone Jabo gave her leads to the blue sky dragon. Perhaps she should feed it to the dragon and be done with the entire ordeal. She knows, though, that Senari's order must be followed. She can kill the dragon, or she can die in Naiwoa. No other options exist. Hoping another will present itself, she drags her chains through the gates of Skyreach Bastion.

F is for Freedom, a lie told by kings, for kingdoms have rulers, and rulers have things.

S<small>KYREACH</small> B<small>ASTION IS A TOWERING FORTRESS CARVED INTO THE BREAST OF THE</small> R<small>OCKFELL</small> P<small>EAKS</small>. Built by master stonemasons, it is fortified by natural cliffs and steep mountains, making it almost impenetrable by outside forces.

The leader of this fortress in the sky believes in a union of strength. Each person represents a single rock that makes up the powerful mountain of Drakhaal. With this strength, they have held off erosion from the inside as well.

Kadara has never held a contract with Torin Halfhammer. His people are safe behind the towering stone walls of the fortress. With large steel bells, they ring the warning of sky dragons and disappear deeper into the mountain until the danger passes. No dragon has ever breached the gates.

No Drakhaalan believes one ever will. Dragonslayers are as needed in Drakhaal as they are in the dragon-less Solmar Desert.

Kadara is led up large steps carved into the mountain; she is pushed and prodded along the way, carrying the bulk of the weight from her chains over her shoulder. Children laugh and scurry about between the prisoners, poking them with sticks and hurling rocks at them. The guards ignore them and push their quarry farther into the mountain. They pass stonemasons at work, a blur of mining tools and climbing harnesses as they labor to refine the stone.

A foundry is pouring steel into molds for the enormous warning bells. Three cast bells sit aside, waiting to be hung from one of the towering belfries high in the mountain stronghold. The thrumming of the forge vibrates the surrounding air at a frequency too low for normal perception. Kadara, though, can hear it reverberate through the bells with as much volume as if Torin's hammer rang them. She winces as the guards push her into an immense stone hall.

Inside the hall, tall, feather-cloaked scholars argue about snowmelt and play Lorgan Dei, an ancient game of chance in which small cubes cut from ice, called "dragons," hide in small wooden sleeves called "caves." Players try to determine which sleeves hold the dragons and which sleeves are safe to "sleep in." The winner is the first to reach three consecutive nights of rest, something Kadara longs for.

Five other prisoners are led in and made to stand beside her, facing an empty throne made of stones of various sizes stacked to resemble a large seat. Four of them sob into each other's shoulders.

The fifth is a proud man with gold inlays highlighting the wave motif on his Naiwoan armor—a Naiwoan knight. He pulls at the others' chains and whispers for them to trust that the river of life will carry them home again. He looks to Kadara for help in calming their fellow captives, but her attention is drawn elsewhere. Her sword is being brought into the hall, along with the weapons of the other prisoners. She can feel its subtle tug as it is wheeled past and set near the throne.

Patience.

The bustling about settles, and onlookers take their seats as Torin Halfhammer enters the echoing hall. His stride is powerful and purposed, sending his floor-length cloak of feathers aflutter as he walks. Torin is the embodiment of physical strength and fortitude, a towering figure, even among the highland people.

His broad, bare shoulders are crisscrossed with deep scars from battles, and the weathering of sunburn earned over years spent swinging his hammer while bathed in light from the Aros sun. The Ologun-made warhammer, Mountainbreaker, hangs from his right hand. His left pulls at the tuft of hair that surrounds his face like the clouds encircling the lofty peaks of Aros. His gray eyes pass over the prisoners and knights alike with the same degree of intrigue.

He reaches the throne, but instead of sitting, he places Mountainbreaker in the seat of honor. The massive hammer seems no less heavy despite the half taken by Kadara's sword long ago.

Kadara ducks her head. Stories of her sword are told in most of Aros to this day, though few would recognize it. This is not most of Aros. This is the Great Hall of Skyreach Bastion, and Torin Halfhammer is known to have a long memory. Kadara tries not to look toward the weapons basket, hoping not to draw notice to the sword. Halfhammer's attention lies elsewhere.

"What happened out there? How is it I see the remnants of battle but not of victory?" His voice is soft, not demanding. He asks aloud as if counseling himself. A Drakhaalan soldier limps forward to speak.

"Drekan the Deceiver." The soldier spits after he says it. "As soon as we charged him on the field of battle, he retreated. As we gave chase, the Naiwoan river scum ambushed us with a sky dragon." The soldier scowls as the proud Naiwoan prisoner interrupts him.

"You called us to battle. You sent us the—"

Torin grabs the shaft of his hammer, silencing the defiant prisoner.

"No," he says. "You say there were three banners?"

The warriors from both kingdoms nod in agreement. "A worthy battle for any dragon worth its scales."

The king of Skyreach Bastion lifts his huge hammer and grimaces. "Drekan the Deceiver called you to battle, fishmonger, not Drakhaal. We descended from the peaks to battle Vulkanar. You crawled from your swamp, it seems, after receiving a message telling you we were coming." He slams the hammer down, shaking the stone chamber. Kadara can hear the bells outside buzzing in response. "Shake the water from your ears. He goaded each of us onto the field of battle all for a chance at his precious blue dragon. Worse, he wet the earth with Drakhaalan blood to bait the trap for his hunt. This in stone, Naiwoan: We will paint the mountainside red with his blood for this."

The Drakhaalan soldiers cheer and stomp as if seeking to bring the mountain down. Torin strides back and forth, pumping his fist and banging his powerful chest. When the roar begins to die, he takes up the hammer and pumps it again to inflate the cacophony. As he does, Kadara glimpses a small gray stone set into a steel band around his wrist. Torin carries an Ileri stone, though his is as dormant as hers had been for all those years. When the roaring calms, Torin continues.

"For now, we have wounded to mend and prisoners to tend to." He looks the prisoners over again, this time with the hammer tight in his grip. Its intricate pattern gleams in the torchlight. He tips over the basket of swords and takes one in his free hand. "Who carries this weapon?" He waits with the patience of a disappointed parent.

The brave knight speaks up.

"I do," he says. Torin tosses it at his feet.

Kadara holds her breath as he reaches to take another from the pile. He grabs a Naiwoan spear.

"And this one?" Torin holds the spear in the air, letting the blade catch the light.

The brave knight speaks again.

"It is mine," he says.

Torin laughs. He gathers the rest of the Naiwoan weapons, leaving Kadara's sword where it lies. One by one, he tosses them at the feet of the brave soldier.

"Let us save some time, shall we? You clearly lead these men, and I can appreciate your taking responsibility for them." He points his massive hammer at the four frightened Naiwoan soldiers. "Scared little chicks," he says, "so very far from the nest. I am not without fairness. You will serve all four sentences for these men." With two precise swings of his hammer, he frees the four prisoners from their chains. "And these chicks will be allowed to fly home."

"No!" The proud Naiwoan lurches at the king, snapping back when he reaches the end of his chain. "They have no weapons. You sentence them to death."

"I have no authority to punish these men as combatants for acts in battle that you yourself have taken responsibility for. They are *not* soldiers, so I cannot take them prisoner. They are not sworn to Drakhaal and therefore have no right to remain in Skyreach Bastion. Perhaps they can hire an escort to get them down the mountain." He pauses, scratching his enormous gray beard in mock ponder. "Though they do not look as though they have anything worthy to trade." He shrugs. "Let us hope they are fleet of foot and remember the safe path down."

With that, he waves his hammer in an arc and brings it down hard to punctuate the ruling. Hammers held by onlookers throughout the hall slam down in response. The four not-soldiers are taken toward the gates, and the proud soldier hurls threats at Torin while being dragged away.

Torin chuckles. His smile is warm, one his people no doubt turn to often in the coldness of the icy peaks. His steely gray eyes fall on Kadara.

"And me?" Kadara lifts her hands to display her heavy manacles.

Torin's smile fades. "And you." He paces, stopping next to her sword. "You are a complicated case. A trespasser with convenient timing. A brave hedge knight 'merely passing through.' Meanwhile, Drakhaalans returning from battle tell a tale of deceit and dragons. They tell a tale of Drekan." He slams his hammer as he says the name. Countless hammers drop around Kadara in anger. "Why are you here, hedge knight?"

Kadara lowers her shackled hands, accepting that no quick release will be coming.

Patience.

"I seek a dragon. Fierce, smart, and as blue as the sky it haunts."

A murmur crawls through the crowd. Torin's smile returns, this time with far less warmth.

"High King Drekan of the Forge has been scouring Aros for a dragon." Torin raises the hammer. "According to the red-robed spies we caught near our gates, the dragon he seeks is 'as blue as the sky.'"

"The red robes are Drekan's assassins," Kadara says, "and I do not work for Drekan."

Torin ignores her.

"Where did you get this sword?" He taps the hilt with his hammer, then uses the hammer and his boot to turn the blade upright.

"It was given to me. Do you know where to find the dragon?"

"I wonder why they refer to him as 'High King.' They have only the one king. No low king, no higher king." Torin takes a rock from the Drakhaal throne and tosses it at the upturned sword. The rock splits against the blade as if it had always been not one but two. A murmur flows through the sea of onlookers again.

"The dragon?" Kadara repeats.

"Drekan lured us onto a three-banner battlefield with the sole purpose of using us as bait for his dragon hunt. So, yes, we know where the blue menace may rest, but since Drekan wishes to know, none shall know but Drakhaal. If he wants the dragon, he can come and get it himself."

"The blue dragon obliterated the Naiwoan forces as well as yours. Queen Senari of the Riverborn has ordered me to find and kill it. If you do not wish to aid me in this quest, then I shall be on my way." Kadara raises the shackles again.

"I might just have it melted down and turned into arrows. I might have those arrows fired from the foggy peaks of Mount Stonegaard into the nothingness beyond." Torin taps the hilt of the sword with his hammer again. Kadara resists the urge to pull it back to her.

"Do as you will, but permit me to leave."

"No. You trespassed on Drakhaal land. We would normally insist on a penalty, but you then aided my men. We insist on a feast."

"I would prefer my sword."

"Don't be rude, outlander. Not to a king. We are all feathers of the same wing here. This in stone. You aided one, you aided us all. The same is true for insults." He tosses another rock onto the blade and watches as it is divided. "Like this insult that you traipsed into the Rockfell Peaks wearing on your back." This time, all hammers fall in unison. "Prepare the feast!" he roars. "Prepare the penalty!"

The crowd of Drakhaalans cries out with him, and the stone walls reverberate with their joy. Kadara watches as long wooden tables float into the hall like river ice, passed upside down from one to the next until in place. Once in position, the tables are flipped and slammed down. Stools come floating in next. Kadara is unshackled and told to find Torin. When she does, they sit across from each other at the end of one of the long tables, Torin's hammer resting at the table's head.

Platters of goat meat and cheeses are passed around with overflowing bowls of steamed root vegetables and brimming tankards of fermented grain and goat's milk. There are no servants in Drakhaal. As a bowl or pitcher is emptied, the person holding it stands, fills it, returns to their seat, and passes the container.

Torin, tending to take a larger share than most, stands to fill one platter, two bowls, and a pitcher before settling in for his meal. Kadara focuses on the vegetables but also enjoys the cheeses and a good deal of the strange ale concoction. When they have almost cleared their plates, Torin shines his warm smile at her.

"What is your name, knight of convenient timing?"

"I am called Kadara."

"Oh? Don't you mean 'Bannerless Kadara'?" His voice is taunting but sharp.

Kadara shifts in her seat, her discomfort rising. Perhaps she should wear a visored helm. The gray hair and weathered skin do nothing to disguise her. "So, you recognize me."

"But of course. Your sword does not claim all your fame." Torin's smile and voice grow. "This, ladies and gentlemen, is the dragonslayer who rode straight into the Battle of Oponroro without taking an oath, took the head of a dragon that had come to feast on combatants, and left without shedding the blood of any warrior on the field."

Kadara remembers that day well. Apparently, so does Torin. His eyes are large, almost doe-like, as they wait for her response.

"It was preying on children."

"It was a glorious battle."

"I had stalked it for weeks."

"And then you simply rode away."

"My task was done." Her voice rises in irritation.

"You could have picked a side." Torin's voice grows louder.

"You won that battle."

"No thanks to you."

"I killed the dragon."

"You should have killed Drekan." He slams the table with a mallet fist. "Which leaves me to wonder: Who tasked you with that dragon? Who sent you here today?" His eyes are no longer round. They have narrowed into slits of keen suspicion.

"I told you I'm not here on behalf of Drekan."

"You do his bidding nonetheless. That in stone." Torin lets the message sink in. "Enough." He waves his large hand in the air. "This wing is strongest when we beat as one. It seems you've earned the favor of some of my men. Thus, you have won your right to trial by Lorgan Dei."

"Lorgan Dei," a returning soldier shouts, a fresh pitcher in her hands.

Torin fills his cup and continues. "This is an altered version, one specific to that damnable sword." He grins at the prospect. "Rather than asking fate which caves hold safety, you'll ask it which bell holds your sword." His grin expands with pride.

"And the ice that is used to play the dragon?" Kadara asks.

"You'll see." He waves in a group of masons who enter, dragging their hasty creation behind them with glee. A long stone table on stone wheels holds three enormous bells. From where Kadara sits, they seem silent. She has grown too accustomed to the ambient ringing of Drakhaal in her short time here. She wonders whether she will hear it long after she leaves.

"Has it been placed?" Torin stands to inspect as the masons nod in unison. He chuckles, a small laugh that Kadara has come to find endearing, and claps his hands. "Don't tell me," he says. "Don't tell me."

As Kadara approaches, the masons explain.

"Only one bell contains The Last Sword of Ologun, lordless one. The others contain nothing," the first of the three masons says, then bows and leaves the hall.

"Should you choose the bell containing the sword, the bell will be lifted, and you will be permitted to leave." The second mason follows his codesigner.

"Should you choose a bell with nothing—"

"I will join the prisoners in the cells, and my sword will become wasted arrows." Kadara finishes for the third mason, who scrunches his face in irritation and leaves the hall.

Torin joins Kadara in front of the bells. "He won't get a chance to present something like this again in his lifetime. You stole his stage from him," he says.

"He would have stumbled over his words, anyway." Kadara smiles despite herself.

"Monster." Torin smiles as well before remembering himself and joining his fellow Drakhaalans at a watching distance. A knight with a waist-length cloak elbows him in the ribs, and they both chuckle. Kadara realizes that the Drakhaalan prisoners are also present. Though stripped of their armor, they are well-fed and clean. The newest of them, the proud Naiwoan, looks on with anger as a Drakhaalan offers him more goat meat.

He takes it and chews with as much indignation as he can muster under such hospitable circumstances. He will likely weep later, thinking about the comfort his men could have had and hoping they made it down the mountain alive. It is doubtful.

When Kadara is ready, she steps toward the bells. The hall is filled with the humming tremor of hammers against the stone floor. She focuses her senses, grateful for the additional vibrations, and listens to the bells before her. They do not ring, despite the hum of hammers. She listens again, thinking herself distracted by the hum, but they do not ring. She steps closer and knocks on the leftmost bell. Its polished surface offers a thud in reply. These bells, Kadara realizes, are made of stone.

She cannot use sound to determine the empty bells from the one containing the sword. Undeterred, she feels for something the observers could not expect. She holds her hand to each bell and concentrates on her sword. The slight tug is only present in the center bell. Kadara steps back from the test and points to the bell in the middle. The crowd is silent. Torin, still ignorant of the correct answer, speaks first.

"Are you certain?"

Kadara nods. The three masons return and stand before three cranks on the opposite side of the stone display. The mason that Kadara interrupted earlier clears his throat while looking at her and speaks.

"We will now lift the bells to reveal the location of the sword. Good luck to the interrupter."

They turn the cranks, and the stone bells rise, revealing three blocks of bright blue ice. Everfrost. In the center block is the sword, contained but irretrievable.

The crowd bursts into laughter. Kadara has won—but not quite. Pulling the sword would have risks. A tiny shard of everfrost could turn into a full tree, spreading icy woe with ease, encompassing her and anyone foolhardy enough to touch her. Kadara's heart is deflated. She had begun to like the mountain dwellers and their charming leader.

"You may take your sword and go." Torin's voice booms throughout the hall and is soon drowned out by a redoubling of laughter and hammer falls at Kadara's expense.

She looks at the king. His giant smile is more playful than mean-spirited, she notices. It widens at the sight of her irritation. To Kadara, he seems to be expecting more. What further punishment could there be? Confused, she turns and looks at the deadly ice block again.

Patience.

She is considering a slow, deliberate pull, maybe from the safe side of a wall, when she sees the everfrost block start to sweat. Her eyes dart back to Torin and his big smile. His face is a sun, his gray hair and beard the rays of a playful star. Kadara smiles back. Everfrost does not sweat. She reaches her scarred hand high into the air and pulls her sword with reckless abandon. The center block bursts into a spray of frost, dust, and ice crystals that sends a panicked scream through the onlookers.

When the panic calms, all wide and blinking eyes take in the sight of Kadara standing with her sword held high and a layer of ice crystals covering her. The skilled masons of Skyreach Bastion had sculpted, polished, and painted blocks of mountain ice to resemble everfrost in the time it took her to argue and feast with their leader.

Torin roars with laughter and pumps his massive hammer in the air to his fellow Drakhaalans' chanting of the dragon-slayer's name.

Kadara smiles and finds the three masons in the crowd. She bows her head in respect. They return the gesture and join the chants.

G is for Greyhaal and ghosts of the past. Hearts heal in the end, but the memories last.

THE SUN DOES NOT RISE IN SKYREACH BASTION. Still, the Drakhaalans do. Like sprouts seeking the light through soil, man, woman, and child rise at dawn and set out to forge a new day, hammers in tow. Kadara does not mind. She is used to starting her day early to chase the sun to the well and fetch water while the dew burns away from the soft, green grass. No grass grows in Skyreach Bastion. No dew-kissed emerald blankets exist on which to lie and watch the light creep across the countryside.

What the Drakhaalans lack in fields, they more than make up for in family. Here, no one picks plump apples or drinks the spring rain or tracks rabbits that have stolen from their gardens. Here, though, no one is alone.

Kadara joins a rockslide of hungry bellies descending to the main hall for a morning meal.

While they eat, Kadara asks again about the blue dragon. This time, Torin agrees to help, after some goading from his soldiers, and sits with Kadara to discuss.

"You are certain that the dragon came north from the battle in Naiwoa?"

Kadara nods, her mouth full of cheese.

"And none saw it on the approach to the gates of Skyreach Bastion?"

She shakes her head no, smiling at the exchange.

Torin smiles his warm smile back and continues. "No. Well, then it should have been seen by our sky watchers. You would have heard the bells ringing. This wretched dragon is cunning. It must have crept low through the shadow of Mount Stonegaard and sought refuge where no eyes could lie upon it. Even ours. Your dragon rests at Fortress Lake."

Others at the table nod and grunt in agreement. Kadara empties a pitcher of sweetened goat's milk and stands to refill it.

"Then I travel to Fortress Lake," she says when she returns.

"Unless you can fly, there is only one way to Fortress Lake." Torin shrugs as he responds, his massive shoulders like loose boulders teetering on a cliff's edge.

"Skyrun River."

"No, but I'm impressed by your knowledge of the region." He raises the pitcher as he speaks and pours a slow stream of goat's milk into his cup. "Fortress Lake feeds Skyrun River with a waterfall taller than the towers of Skyreach Bastion." He lengthens the pour for added effect before setting the pitcher down. "Long before the dragons came, our people made a home there, and protected by waterfall and mountain, we built a fortress. When the dragons came, we fled deeper into the mountains and built this stronghold to survive.

"We visit Fortress Lake no more. To do so is forbidden to Drakhaalans. To do so, you must awaken the ghosts of promises long past. From long before we were Drakhaalans. To reach Fortress Lake, you must travel through the darkened corridors of Greyhaal."

"Greyhaal," a soldier calls from the end of the table. Hammers around the hall meet the stone in solemn acknowledgement. Torin continues.

"When our people fled the dragons, a strong wizard fled with us. She was called Lilo Kuta, and she sacrificed herself to see that Drakhaal came to be. She ushered our people to safety and sealed the tunnel behind us. It is said that when she sealed the tunnel, she made our people promise never to go back. The gray Ileri stone glowed for three whole days, and Lilo Kuta was never seen again."

Kadara is motionless. Torin's stone glowed just as hers does.

"If you find her ghost roaming those halls," he says, "tell her she is loved. Tell her we sing her name in songs of battle. Tell her that every year, we light a fire so large the Sharu'un can see it from the far reaches of the Solmar Desert. Let her know it glows for three whole days."

Hammers strike the ground again, jolting Kadara. She looks at the gray Ileri stone on Torin's wrist, feeling the warm light beneath her armor and wondering if a connection exists. These murky questions must wait. The path forward is clear. She will breach the halls of Greyhaal and find her way to Fortress Lake.

Kadara follows Torin through the tall, echoing corridors of the stronghold. As they walk, the air seems to thicken around them, compressed by the ever-tightening halls they traverse. The people, in contrast, loosen like gravel beneath careless feet. When the bodies have thinned so that Kadara can count the puzzled eyes following them without needing extra fingers, Torin pulls a torch from the wall and hands it to her. He pulls another for himself.

"Come. We shouldn't hesitate. It will only make things worse." He motions, and Kadara follows him through the parting darkness to a stone wall set deep in the mountain. Carved into the wall is a doorframe complete with a stone door, lock, and handle. Kadara kneels and peers through a hollow keyhole. Only darkness waits on the other side. She steps back and looks at Torin, who is hesitant to look at the strange archway. He hands her his torch and takes his hammer in both hands.

"I can wait for the dragon to leave." She can feel his discomfort. Despite their rough introduction, she now sees Torin as an ally, a friend.

"Drekan won't be goading anyone into a fight for a while, not after his latest treachery. That dragon could stay at Fortress Lake forever. As much as it would please me, err, Drakhaal, to have you as a more permanent guest, you have a contract to fulfill. Besides," he says, raising Mountainbreaker high in the air, "the last thing this kingdom needs is a local dragon." With that, he brings the hammer down with substantial force. "One strike to release the lock; another to reset it."

A burst of cold air pushes through the nigh-invisible space beyond the carved doorframe, dousing the torches. The stone door shudders and sinks into the floor beneath it. Torin steps back, his eyes down. "I peered through the keyhole as a child. Most of the bravest of us did, but one should never peer with both eyes directly into yesterday." He lifts his hammer again without lifting his gaze. "Go. Should you return to this doorway, call for me. Someone will hear, and I will release the lock once more. Should you not return, I will mourn you. You are always welcome in Drakhaal, Dragonslayer Kadara."

"Thank you, Torin." She sets the extinguished torches down and steps through the ancient doorway and into the labyrinth beyond. "It is nice to have friends in high places."

Kadara can hear Torin's chuckle and the hammer's strike on the stone as she enters the tunnels. The stone doorway grinds back into place, leaving her standing in what feels like an even deeper darkness. She tugs at the chain holding her amulet, and the blue Ileri stone springs free from hiding, illuminating the long-sleeping walls around her in its soft blue light. Ahead of her, the tunnel has collapsed. Large stones and rubble block the path forward. Kadara is not deterred. She cuts away at the blockade, opening a pathway more and more with each blow of her sword.

When the effort blinds her eyes with sweat, she takes a break, leaning against the stone wall and thinking of the cool wind that blows by her hilltop cottage. She longs for home, but given that she has been arrested twice for trespassing since leaving her holding, she wonders if it has become more a prison than a refuge. Unsworn knights were free to wander when she was adventuring. Borders meant a change of opportunity, not a chance of imprisonment. So much has changed in a world that seems otherwise the same.

When the thumping of her taxed heart quiets, she starts again. Piece by piece, she cuts away stones as thick as her sword is long and pushes them behind her. When she pauses, thinking she may need to rest again, a loosened stone lets through a gust of stale air. She cuts away enough room to slip through without removing her armor and enters Lilo Kuta's labyrinth. The ghost of a voice from long ago seems to whisper in her ear.

"Go," it says. "Don't turn back, and always stay together..."

"They made it to Drakhaal, Lilo," Kadara whispers, "and they live today as one."

The blue light of the stone cannot reach deep enough into the dark depths of the hall ahead. Kadara pulls an unlit torch from the wall. Cobwebs break away and the dust of long settled memories floats about. She strikes her sword against the wall at an angle, sending sparks toward her new light source. It flares a cool green, then burns yellow before deciding that orange is the color it always aspired to be.

She takes another torch from the wall and touches it to the lit one. It, too, settles on orange. Kadara tosses it down the hall ahead of her. The orange glow paints the tunnel, revealing a series of side passages. Beside each passage is a wall torch. She smiles. This is not her first labyrinth.

***

Kadara has visited three labyrinthine corridors prior to this one. Orun Jabo had insisted on it as vehemently as he would later insist that she go to Ologun for his sword. Jabo walked her through each labyrinth, explaining the pitfalls and pointing out the telltale signs of traps and exits. While most of her lessons were learned alone, Jabo insisted on joining her for these, saying it gave him a chance to visit old friends. He was a jovial mentor but a difficult one. When Kadara first came to him to study, he turned her away.

"Kill a thing for what it does," Jabo had said then, "not for what it is." He said this always. He said it when he first turned her away. He said it when she, after their long mentorship, left his care, a full-fledged dragonslayer with no interest in killing. Jabo was right, of course. Dragons require solitude and peace. They require food and water and materials to form their eggs. They require room to roam. Like bears and wolves and mountain lions, dragons kill to survive. Humans kill for other reasons.

Over the years, Kadara has slayed far more humans than dragons. Often for the very behavior that dragons are hunted for.

When Jabo had agreed to mentor her at last, he explained that, unlike defending one's self from it, the use of magic was not something a wizard could teach. "Some wizards do not even know where the magic comes from," he told her with laughing eyes. What he could teach her, however, was the recognition of magic. He could teach her to see when it was being used. "Wizard magic and dragon magic are the same, for there is only one magic—the magic of Aros. To recognize wizard magic is to recognize the lights and lines of dragon magic."

The first labyrinth had been troublesome for Kadara. Jabo walked in with her and disappeared as soon as he could. When she turned to find him, she saw that the entrance had disappeared as well. She could hear his voice but could do nothing to see him or determine where he stood. As she walked about the maze, she lit torches, but Jabo followed in her wake with a gentle breeze that put them out before she rounded a corner. When her feet grew tired, she called out to the wizard for help. Orun Jabo revealed himself and asked her what he could help with.

"Release me from this maze, and I will try again tomorrow."

"You are not locked in here, Dragonslayer," Orun Jabo said. "This place has no bars, no doors."

Kadara rolled her eyes.

"I wish to leave this place."

"Then leave."

"I cannot."

"Why?"

"I do not know where I am."

"Why not?"

"You erased the signs of where I have been."

"I suspect you never knew where you were going."

"Guide me from this place, wizard."

"I cannot."

"Why not?"

"Because I followed you in."

"So, you are lost with me?"

"If you are lost, then so am I."

"This is not a very good lesson, Jabo."

"I've certainly learned a few things. I won't be following you into labyrinths, for one."

"Jabo!" But the wizard's smile was infectious. His big, toothy grin could do more to solve Aros's woes than all the magic he could conjure. Kadara smiled despite her anger and waited for the lesson to reveal itself.

"Think, Kadara. What magic binds us here?"

"A wizard's magic," she said, uncertain.

"Which is?"

"Akin to dragon magic."

"And what can a dragon do?"

She thought for a moment. Dragon magic varies, but there are clear limitations. Dragons are impervious to fire. Dragonfire, everfrost, flight, and invisibility are established skills, but none of them could explain her imprisonment. She smiled back at the wizard, an answer on her tongue.

"Shapeshifting," she said.

"That is correct." The wizard pointed to the end of the hall and laughed. A new series of halls had appeared before them. Kadara took a step toward the newest corridor, but Jabo held her arm. "Only a wizard can craft a labyrinth, and only once. The act of doing so is the ultimate sacrifice. It kills the wizard." He said that last part as if the words were too heavy for the breath he could provide. "What is the purpose of a labyrinth, Kadara?"

Her first thought told her it was to trap people, but she knew that was a mistake, too simple. A labyrinth is not designed to trap *everyone*. In fact, its purpose is not to trap at all but to prevent passage.

"A labyrinth prevents certain people from passing through." She shrugged, uncertain what the epiphany afforded her.

Jabo, though, lit up like a wall torch. He shook her hand, something he did often, and thanked her for the lesson. Though she wanted to pry the rest of it from him, she knew that attempting to do so would only lengthen the wait. Patience was the sole key to Jabo's tongue. When the wait had grown so long that it appeared he had forgotten their predicament, he turned to Kadara and continued.

"What is at the end of this labyrinth, Kadara?" He asked the question with an innocence that suggested Kadara had brought him here as his teacher and not the other way around.

"I do not know, Jabo." Kadara peered down the long, endless maze of halls as if an answer would appear. When it did not, she sighed. "I don't really care."

"Neither do I. We should just leave, don't you think?"

Kadara smiled. She understood at last. Turning to face the hall they had come down, she took Orun Jabo's hand and started toward the original entrance. As though understanding their intentions, it appeared before them: the only true exit.

"No reason to keep us," Jabo said with a hearty laugh, "not if we don't intend to take anything with us. As it is with all magic in Aros. Consider, if you will, Kadara, that all magic is meant to protect. It becomes very dangerous for those who seek to subvert it."

Twice more they had found labyrinths. Twice more they had ventured in for as long as they could stand it and then turned back and exited the mesh of twisted halls with ease. Whatever each maze hid was safe from them, and they were free to leave, a gateway forming to meet their goals.

***

The memory melts away like sun-beaten snow. Kadara smiles.

"That was an excellent lesson, Jabo."

The torches flicker and a cool breeze caresses her face. Ahead of her, sunlight teases at the entrance to the maze. Lilo Kuta created this labyrinth to hide Drakhaal. Exiting to Fortress Lake will be easy, but once she goes, Kadara can never find her way back. Not this way. The Greyhaalan wizard, Lilo, had seen to that.

"One thing at a time," Kadara says as she marches toward the light. "One thing at a time."

The amulet heats the surface of Kadara's armor as she passes through the mouth of the labyrinth and into the stronghold once known as Greyhaal. She tucks it away and takes in her surroundings. The tall, intricate pillars resemble the architecture of Drakhaal, with its sweeping lines and carved archways.

Here, though, time has not been kind. Like a lie heard once too many times, the damage has found an entrance and taken root. Windblown snow and age-old dust coat every surface. The remains of abandoned, disintegrating eagles' nests wait above almost every doorway. Wool bedding, likely for a family of goats, lies crumpled in a darkened corner. Kadara steps around it and into the ancient hall, her sword at the ready. Crumbled walls and toppled columns greet her, and she follows the wind and the light until she reaches a breach in the western wall. Beyond it, she can see a vast stretch of ice surrounded by tall trees and mountains.

Nothing but snow rests in the center of Fortress Lake. The dragon may have been there but taken flight as Kadara stole through Greyhaal to meet it. With no intention of attempting a return through Lilo's labyrinth, Kadara raises her sword and slices at the wall, widening the breach. The crisp mountain air kisses her face and hair with soft ice crystals, the amulet melting any snow before it can settle on her cuirass. Its warmth heightens with each step as she makes the short trek from the fortress ruins to the lakefront. She steps into the basin, her amulet scorching her chest, and walks along the edge of the frozen lake, searching for signs of the dragon.

The dragon finds her instead.

H is for Heart, pumping blood through the veins. As long as it's beating, you'll live through the pain.

THE DRAGON BURSTS FORTH FROM BENEATH THE ICE, A RISING CLOUD OF FROST AND FURY. Kadara sees the whole of herself reflected in its huge, golden eye and hesitates. It is only a moment but one too many. A boulder-sized chunk of lake ice comes hurtling toward her. In the blink of an eye, she brings her sword down, hoping to slice through it.

She is successful. The ice is halved.

In the next moment, both pieces hit her as one and send her flying, limp and breathless, away from the frigid waters. She lands hard and slides, gasping to refill her lungs. The dragon screeches in anger, its muscular torso ribboning in the air. This time it remembers her for certain.

"I remember you too," Kadara says, choking as she regains her feet. "I remember what you took from me." She raises a hand to draw the shard from the dragon, but the dragon is ready. It hurls another chunk of ice at Kadara before she can focus in full. This time she sees it coming soon enough to dive out of the way. When she is back on her feet, the dragon is gone from sight.

She reaches once more for the shard, and the dragon responds, bursting through the ice beneath her like a furious, scaled geyser. Kadara is thrown clear again. Before she can hit the ground, the dragon is striking, having turned like a tight riverbend in the air to keep track of its prey. Its vast, toothed jaw snaps closed, just missing Kadara's leg as she kicks free and lands.

The dragon slams into the mountainside behind her from its own momentum, sending rocks and rubble raining down on her head. She shields herself with the sword and cuts her way free in time to see the dragon mounting another charge. "Is the threat of division no deterrent to you, dragon? Let me show you why it should be."

This time, Kadara plants her feet and refuses to move. She holds her sword in front of her, blade out, like a determined and deadly log splitter. The enraged, blue sky terror uncoils like a whip in the air and races toward her. Kadara turns her sword to reflect the sun's rays into the beast's eyes.

The dragon keeps coming, blinded by the light. At the last heartbeat, Kadara falls onto her back and traces a line down the dragon's underside with her sword.

As the dragon's tail whips by, Kadara rolls and looks up at her attacker. The dragon is unfazed. She goads it again, flashing the light into its eyes and slicing at its scaly underbelly as it passes. The sword cannot break its hide. Kadara rolls once more, cursing at the dragon and drawing at the shard. The dragon writhes in the air and slams into the ice, sending chunks flying toward the dragonslayer.

Kadara dodges the debris with ease, slicing at the last chunk to be certain her sword still works as it should. It cuts like a knife through Drakhaalan cheese, and Kadara looks back at the dragon, frustrated and confused. She can hear its frantic breathing, smell the brimstone as it prepares a volley of dragonfire. She can smell something more there as well—something familiar. The dragon lets loose a barrage of sticky, explosive embers, and Kadara takes a path around the lake, sprinting, dodging, and hoping for enough time to understand her dilemma.

The dragon is relentless. It keeps a constant, fiery pursuit while using its tail to whip icy shards from the surface of the lake into Kadara's path. After a while, the luck of the dragon wins out, and a shard of ice clips her heel. She spins hard into a snowdrift, the sharp edge of her sword pressed against her face. It pushes into her skin as she slides it from beneath her and rolls onto her back. The sword has never cut her. It never will.

"It's in your blood," she says as the dragon pounces. Kadara hasn't been pulling at the sword's shard but at the bloodstream of the great and mighty beast. Just as it became one with her when pressed into her wound, the dragonstone has been absorbed by the beast's hot blood. Kadara cannot hurt this dragon with her sword any more than she could hurt herself. She has lost.

The dragon pins her arms and its head draws close, a predator eyeing its prey before the slaughter. Satisfied it has won the day, it rears back and releases a terrifying roar. Kadara remembers the smell now. It is in the smell of her hair when she cuts it in springtime. It is in the taste of her blood when she pricks her finger on a rose. It is in the scent of her frosty breath on winter mornings. Understanding this is an odd mixture of comforting and terrifying. For the dragon, it has been agony.

The enraged beast finishes its battle cry and spits up the belly of blue fire it has been brewing over the helpless dragonslayer. The hot magma muffles Kadara's scream, pouring into her throat. She breaks free of the dragon's grasp and rolls, coughing and spitting, toward the lake.

With her sword still grasped to defend herself, she realizes the dragonfire has not harmed her. Her armor is not so lucky. She rises, much to the dragon's surprise, and looks from its puzzled face to the icy waters, her armor crackling and threatening to fail. With nothing to lose, she abandons all caution and dives into the icy depths of Fortress Lake. The dragon gives chase.

The lake is deeper than Kadara expected. She curses herself for not remembering that an entire dragon recently hid beneath its ice, but she never has time to reach the bottom. The dragon catches up with her, its mouth wide, and clamps down. Its great fangs tear into the front of Kadara's armor, crushing her, and forcing out what little breath remains in her lungs. While grasping her sword, she pulls hard at the dragon's blood.

With Kadara still clenched in its teeth, the creature explodes from the water, slashing and flailing in pain, but it does not release its grip. Kadara pulls again, harder this time, and the frantic dragon flies headlong into a Greyhaalan pillar. The force of the blow wrenches Kadara free, and she gasps for air, clawing at her chest. The cuirass has been ripped from her body, become lodged in the teeth of her ferocious attacker. Her breath is growing shallow, her consciousness fading.

Get up, Kadara, she tells herself. *Get up.* Images of home flash through her rattled mind as she grasps for balance, teetering between being alert and asleep. *The apples are ripening on the branch,* she thinks, pushing herself. *If they fall, they will rot where they lie.*

The dragon frees the breastplate from its fangs and prepares for another attack.

Pick yourself up, woman. Do not lie in wait for rot to come. Using her sword as a crutch, Kadara forces herself into a hunched standing position.

The azure Ileri stone swings from her neck, a searing beacon of soft blue light. She hears the dragon's scales rubbing together as it coils for a final strike.

"Fine, then," she calls out. "Let us be done with it." She stiffens her back, stretching into a proud standing position, and stares down the charging dragon. It stares right back, bathed in the blue light of the Ileri stone, and charges. It flies right into the glow of the amulet. Its eyes, this time, look somehow different, almost human. Before Kadara can verify this with her own failing eyes, the pain overcomes her and darkness seeps into her mind.

Kadara dreams of Orun Jabo's laughing eyes.

"Slay a thing for what it does, not for what it is," he says.

When Kadara wakes, the dragon is carrying her in one of its gigantic claws. It grips her sword in another. The dragon winds through the sky, high in the clouds, like a deadly whipfish swimming through the air. Kadara tries to call her sword, but the veil of dreaming responds instead.

I is for Island. Secluded, alone. The sharpness of solitude cuts to the bone.

KADARA WAKES ON A STONEY BEACH, SALTWATER RUSHING IN AROUND HER. She sees her sword lying a few feet away and scrambles for it before realizing she has been left alone. A rocky cliffside crowns the beach, the incoming tide approaching low as if bowing. Kadara rises and climbs to relative safety, listening to the world around her. She hears insects and some small game skittering through the brush but nothing more. Looking out over the water, she sees distant glaciers and hears sea lions barking. A whale sprays somewhere to the west.

Well above the tide line, she ventures farther inland, following the rise of the land until she reaches a point high enough to see more of her surroundings. To the south, she sees the curving shore of northern Teyhala, leading into what must be the Alawhe Inlet. The dragon has flown her to Alawhe Island.

She watches the tide between the island and mainland rush by. The choppy waters would devour any canoe she could build within seconds of launching. The swim would be impossible. Through eyes focused by her amulet's power, the mainland shore of Teyhala looks dark and desolate. Kadara can see no activity to offer encouragement, and the Teyhalans only dock their fleet once a year. She is not lucky enough to have been stranded at that time. They frequent the home waters when at sea, though, so with any luck, she'll be able to signal a passing ship.

From her perch at the top of the hill, Kadara estimates the size of the island. From the low beach to the northern cliffs, it is about three days of walking and climbing, given the terrain. Unlike the short, sweet journeys to the market from her cottage, this one would take a great deal of apples. She decides to set up camp here, where she can spot approaching vessels.

She lifts the amulet and spins it, gauging the direction of the dragon. A faint signal comes from the south. She is far from her strange captor but feels close. Only two creatures in all of Aros hold dragonstone in their blood, to her knowledge. Until a short time ago, Kadara had thought herself the only one. That the dragon she was sent to kill cannot kill her, or be killed by her sword, is a malicious game for fate to play.

Kadara scans the horizon and sets to work creating a shelter. The tall trees fall like shorn grass to her blade, and she planes them with ease, leaving long, flat boards to lean against each other like a wooden tent. With little effort, she weaves tall island grasses into a waterproof cover for the shelter.

What remains of her armor is battered and dented. She removes it, chooses the parts that still have some shine to them, and places them on wooden pikes in a circle around her hilltop bivouac, hoping they will catch the light as a ship goes by. She braids the singed leather straps from her greaves and bracers together as a belt to keep her tunic from billowing in the northern wind.

When the tide rolls out again, Kadara drags deep trenches into the rocky sand with the Worldsunderer, like furrows between the rows in her garden. The trenches reveal buried gastropods. They will be her sustenance until she can figure out how to fashion a fishing net. She collects long, flat strips of seaweed from the wave-kissed rocks along the shore and stores them in the shade of her shelter. At regular intervals, she scans the horizon with eyes and ears to pick out any sign of a Teyhalan ship. When night rolls over the face of the water, she starts a fire and feeds it until she falls asleep.

Once the morning sun peeks through the small entrance to her temporary home, Kadara rises and sets to work weaving a net from the seaweed. She uses her basket-making technique and weaves the net wider and wider as she turns the seaweed. The strips break away as she bends them for knots, so she moves to the shore and loosens the fibers with seawater. The knots tighten like leather as they dry, giving her a more secure hold than she had hoped for.

While she works, she travels back and forth from shoreline to camp to keep the fire burning low and feeds it wet grass from time to time to ensure a steady rise of white smoke. When the net is finished and she is satisfied it will hold fish, she rests beside the fire until the tide is high. After a quick scan of the horizon, Kadara heads to the cliff's edge above the low beach and casts her stone-weighted net out over the water.

Only two corners sink; the other two are buoyed by hollowed-out wood.

Kadara goes back to the tent and tends to the smoke signal while she waits for the tide to roll out. When it does, she returns to the beach to collect the bounty of fish trapped in her net.

Barking sea lions crowd the beach. As she approaches, she sees they have torn through her net and devoured her fish.

"No," she says, as if speaking to children.

The sea lions bark louder.

"Please leave."

They charge at her, for they are many, and she is alone. She backs away until her shoulders press against the mossy cliffside. "I have no wish to hurt you."

They bark louder, stomping the sand and bobbing about. This is their island. She is not welcome here. When Kadara is certain they will attack, they turn, cross the beach, and dive into the water.

Kadara has frightened animals before. This is not of her doing, and her sword is at her camp.

It rests beside a ring of stones that houses her fire and mimics the shape of the armor ring she placed around her tent. A ship could easily spot the gleaming ring of armor once close enough.

Distance is far less limiting for dragons.

Her amulet sings the soft song of a far-off dragon. The sea lions bark the panicked barks of a present one. She runs toward the water. Dragonfire follows.

Many are the orphans of Aros. Most often, they are the children of warriors who never made it home with their promised glory. Kadara was one such child. Too young to remember her parents, she slept in the schoolhouse with the other orphans. When she was old enough to hold a sword, the school pushed her from the nest and told her to find her way in the world. Such is Aros: a cradle made of fire to lie in all alone.

When she is far enough from the cliffside to evade the dragonfire, Kadara spins and pulls hard, calling her sword. On the cliff above her, a dragon the pale yellow of cloudy mornings screeches and takes to the sky. Kadara pulls again, and the dragon spins in the air, revealing its back and her sword buried in it. The sword comes free and falls to the rocky sand below. She pulls once more, this time catching the sword in her grasp, and sprints toward the path to the camp. The dragon lands hard behind her, twisting and roaring, blood pouring from the wound in its spiked spine. It whips a long, mace-like tail at the hedge knight, but Kadara is ready and cuts through it with a grunting swing. The dragon screeches again and returns to the air, this time to flee.

Alone again, Kadara jogs up the path to her ravaged camp. The armor has been devoured; the shelter, burned. She sighs and sits in the ruins, more disappointed in her shortsightedness than in the loss of the armor. Smoke will still serve as a signal, and dragons are not likely to come to inspect it.

Weeks turn into months while Kadara enjoys relative peace and waves to the whales that swim by. The seasons seldom change this far north, but storms come and go more often than not. Kadara counts the storms until she forgets how many have passed and laughs at the idea of keeping time in a place like this.

Fish oils and a carved wooden comb keep her hair from locking, and she lets it grow long enough for her braid to pass her shoulders for the first time in years. She carves new animals from deadfall and driftwood, careful to hide them among the trees to avoid dragon encounters. They are far smaller than the carvings that Ologun surrounded her cottage with, but they are a welcome reminder of home. All the while, she looks to the skies for the blue dragon. If it ever comes, the amulet does not notice, happy to hum away in a dull hint of acknowledgement.

Fresh fish, mussels, and seaweed keep her full and happy. Having seen her protect the island, the sea lions leave her to it as if they see it as her holding and refuse to trespass. An eagle visits at the end of one cloudy day, and Kadara thinks of Torin and the Drakhaalans deep in the mountain. It has been, she realizes, the better part of a year since she left the gracious highlanders. She hopes they do not mourn her and makes a promise to herself to visit them before returning to her hilltop holding on the mainland for good.

The likelihood of that seems as far-off and hidden as the blue dragon, so she distracts herself by scanning the never-ending line between the sky and sea for ships. Today, for the first time since waking on the island, she sees a tiny dot on the horizon that doesn't disappear beneath the waves.

Kadara tosses driftwood, held at the ready for such an occasion, over the flames to stoke the fire, then steps away from the crackling embers of the fire and listens in the direction of the dot. With the amulet enhancing her hearing, she catches the resonant ringing of a whipfish flute and yelps in glee.

White smoke climbs into the sky as she stuffs wet grass into the glowing embers. Laughing, she peers eagle-eyed at the shape on the water. It grows in a gradual expansion, easing closer like a storm cloud. Two monstrous sails, like gigantic lungs, hold and harness the wind, the Teyhalan Trident emblazoned on them. Kadara tosses what remains of her grass onto the smoking fire and watches the billows rise like a flock of seagulls.

Once satisfied the ship is turning toward Alawhe Island, she kicks dirt over the fire to extinguish it, pulls her sword to her hand, and makes her way to the northern shore. Her amulet remains idle, but she tucks it into her tunic nonetheless, choosing caution over carelessness.

When the ship nears, Kadara turns her sword in the sunlight to signal it. She listens to the ship's sounds and among them hears the clinking chains of a falling anchor, the splash of a rowboat landing on the water's surface, and a familiar voice. Admiral-Knight Rodahn warns his shipmates to use caution as they do not know who is on the island. With a smile that shines with as much brilliance as her armor once had, Kadara tosses her sword into the sea and dives in after it.

She meets the island-bound rowboat where the tidal waters begin pulling toward Alawhe Inlet. Panting for air but still smiling, she reaches her hand out to one of her confounded rescuers. The Teyhalan sailor takes it but hesitates.

"Where is your weapon?" he asks as she places her free hand on the rim of the boat. "The one you signaled us with."

"She threw it in the water," his boatmate says.

"Fine," the suspicious sailor says and pulls her onboard.

Once in the small boat, Kadara sits near the bow, where the outstretched spears of her saviors are less likely to prod her.

"Why were you on Alawhe?" the sailor asks.

They are like man-shaped oceans, calm on the surface but teeming with energy below. She listens to their hearts beating and chuckles when direct eye contact quickens the observant sailor's pulse.

"I was stranded," Kadara says.

The spears remain pointed at her face.

"Why did you signal Teyhala?"

"I was stranded." She raises a hand to indicate the island, as if to demonstrate her situation with a visual aid.

The sailors look at each other, at the island, and back at Kadara. They lower their spears a hair and lean their heads together to confer in whispers. Kadara listens.

"What should we do?" the suspicious sailor asks.

"You should take me to Admiral-Knight Rodahn," Kadara says. The spears float back up to eye level, heartbeats thrumming in alarm.

"Row," says the observant sailor.

Kadara nods and raises her hand. She nudges the spears from her face and takes the oars. In swift, confident strokes, she pulls at them, gliding the boat across the water like the fin of a confident shark. Her obvious strength does nothing to put the sailors at ease. Neither does the rowboat's path: It approaches the ship, one that is identical to every other ship in the fleet, in a straight, deliberate line.

When they arrive, hooks are lowered, and Kadara attaches them to the boat while the sailors keep their spears trained on her. Thick, mossy ropes hoist the small craft, and the sailors climb out. Kadara waits in her seat, hands on her lap.

When the sailors deliver word to Rodahn of the peculiar castaway, Kadara hears his hearty laugh. She chuckles at her strange, tidal luck. How it always seems to ebb and flow. The skies are clear, and a soft breeze brushes against her cheek as the sun tries in vain to dry her dripping tunic. Even the elements sometimes struggle to achieve their goals.

Rodahn approaches and goads her at once, showing he remembers their brief time together with the same fondness she does.

"So, it's serial trespassing for you, then?"

Kadara tries and fails to hide her smile. "I wanted to give you another chance to free me from imprisonment." She stands and turns to face him. He is still in his Naiwoan armor, a set of throwing knives tucked into his belt. Kadara notices a new trinket around his neck, beside his river stone and the worn shell she saw before. A dormant, dark purple Ileri stone catches the sun's light.

"The first time was more impressive," she says.

Rodahn lets out his signature laugh, and the onlooking sailors join him.

"Permission to board?"

The laughter stops. A deluge of whispers washes over the ship as Kadara bathes in a sea of surprised eyes. Most who live on land do not know of this Teyhalan custom. Having traveled a great deal of the six kingdoms in her storied youth, Kadara is well acquainted.

"For that honor, you'll have to ask my sister." Rodahn steps aside to reveal the pearl he and his men have formed a protective shell around. "Admiral-Queen Kala of the Deep."

"May the wind fill her sails," the sailors say as one, and the ruler of Teyhala steps forward.

Kala is tall and regal, with an athletic build honed by years at sea. Her purple-dyed hair, short and thick, glistens in the sun like the surface of the ocean. From striking violet eyes, a sharp, calculating gaze falls on Kadara like a rain of arrows. Kala shifts her gaze to her brother, who seems more than prepared to let loose another laugh, and rolls her eyes.

"Granted," she says, and the suspicious sailor who pulled Kadara from the water reaches out his hand to help her aboard. Kadara accepts the help and thanks Kala for her generosity. A generosity that she can see spread to the other faces on board.

Only Rodahn wears armor, looking as comfortable blanketed in steel as he is holding it. Everyone else wears the sleek, form-fitting skins of Teyhala. Made to repel water and keep sailors warm in the brisk sea air, these garments are woven from animal hide but resemble the vibrant fabrics seen at the market Kadara once frequented.

Dyes of all colors differentiate the sailors of one Teyhalan ship from another, Kadara knows. On Kala's ship, the royal standard of purple is displayed throughout, with exceptions made for undyed grays, blacks, and browns. Whisker-thin threads cut from the coats of seals allow the wearer to enter the water without the risk of sinking that would accompany heavy armor or waterlogged robes.

Kala's face shifts from calculating to amused as Kadara works to find her footing. Kadara smiles back, intoxicated by the idea of having left the island.

She has traded wind in her hair and salt spray on her face for more of the same, but it feels good to be moving again. She reaches her hand over the side of the ship and snatches her sword from the depths with a flick of her wrist.

Rodahn laughs, and Kala joins him despite herself. "Is she a wizard?" she asks.

"No," Rodahn says, "but Senni called her a dragonslayer."

Kala initiates the laughing this time. "Even better."

She walks away as if floating, the sway of the ship seeming to leave her to her whims, and disappears into the sea of sailors, the flow of her path marked only by the movement of her spearhead above the crowd.

"Come, Dragonslayer, we will have wine and words in my cabin."

Kadara drips as she follows Kala, her bare feet leaving footprints on the polished deck.

"We'll get you a change of clothes as well. Do not worry, I want nothing from you save what is certain to be a worthy tale."

They disappear below decks, Rodahn's laughter and orders ringing behind them.

Kadara accepts a hodge-podge garment of tightly woven black sealskin that fits like her armor once did and protects her much the same. She thanks the tailor with so much sincerity that he fashions a pocket in the front to hold her amulet and weaves her hair into eight splendid braids. They run in even rows along her scalp and either coil down her back or over her shoulders. With the flecks of gray throughout, the braids look like foam-tipped waves dancing on the night sea.

When they are seated in her quarters, Kala pours two glasses of rich Moanaake wine and motions to a set of wooden chairs. A long trident with prongs made from a gleaming, sea-blue metal, each tip sharp enough to pierce ship hulls, leans against the wall. The shaft is wrapped in coral and ocean stones, giving it a natural yet regal appearance, like it was pulled from the deepest depths of the sea. Kadara takes a glass and sits down. She drinks the wine and sighs in satisfaction. Kala joins her and drinks a deep swig of wine as well.

"It is said that in all the world, there is only water, sky, and Aros," Kala says. "Long before the First Battle and the appearance of the Dragon's Grasp, a different rising occurred, and Aros sprang forth from the sea as fire and stone and smoke and fury. When the magic finally settled, there was Aros—the Mother's Womb. Who is to say, though, that no other land exists? It is out there, and Teyhala will find it and the magic that it hides."

"And then?"

"And then we sail again."

They laugh and touch their glasses together.

"I have heard this desire spoken by many Teyhalans," Kadara says. "I doubt I would hear it from the mouth of Rodahn. He seems more suited for battle than discovery. Still, you must be very proud."

Kala nods and sets her glass down.

"Battle has long since drained from the Teyhalan veins. His blood runs hotter than most land-walkers. He is one of the greatest warriors in all of Aros, unmatched in his mastery of weapons. With him at my side, I could retake all Teyhalan land, from Deepwater Hold to Otun Lake. Do you know why I do not?" She turns her head as if presenting an ear for Kadara to pour her answer into.

"Because Teyhala needs no land."

Kala smiles and nods.

"There are a thousand ships sailing the shores of Aros. They are all Teyhalan. The other five rulers do not just share borders with my kingdom; they are *surrounded* by it. Teyhala controls the water. Teyhala controls the sea." She finishes her glass of wine and pours another.

"And the partnership with Naiwoa?" Kadara raises an eyebrow.

Kala scoffs.

"Yes, there lies my pride." She pours Kadara another glass. "Ro is amphibious. Even as a boy, he had one foot on dry land. Thanks to his political acumen, Teyhala trades with every kingdom save Vulkanar."

"Vulkanar does not trade."

"Not yet. Rodahn will not give up, though." Kala's laughter is like tiny bells tumbling along the deck of a ship. "When I first agreed to let him parlay with Naiwoa, it was in the hope that another water-faring nation would see value in our shipbuilding and trade for the grains that our loss of land denies us. King Jor refused my requests for so very long that I was prepared to trade with the Sharu'un of the Solmar Desert instead. Ro's magic tongue and obvious skill in battle secured trade deals with both and more. He will never be king of his people. Ruling is something he is happy to ensure I can do for a long time. What Rodahn commands, what he is lord of, is the battlefield. He has done more for Teyhala than I ever could and wants nothing in return save for the prosperity of his people and the occasional cause to swing his blade."

Kadara clinks her glass against her host's.

"And you? What is it that you want?"

A heavy silence falls over the cabin. When Kala speaks again, it is in a near whisper.

"As the first born to the Admiral-King, I was always going to be queen, be it on land or at sea. While Ro was being taught how to defend Teyhala, I was being raised to take it back. When our father died, I abandoned his goals. It nearly tore the fleet apart. For me, Teyhala will never be a stretch of land with a sacred stronghold. What we already have is sacred; it is what no other nations do: a stretch of water leading to wonders no one has ever seen. I would die to keep Teyhala free." She sips her wine, a thoughtful look painting her face as she swallows.

"I nearly did so as well, by the hands of some of the very people that I was born to lead. When you are raised on the sea, it is easy to forget that some long for stable ground. My decision was final and will remain so as long as I draw breath." She pauses to refill their glasses while posing a question. "How far out have you been?"

"On the sea?" Kadara shrugs. "Alawhe Island."

Kala nods.

"And that is farther than most will ever go. You see, the ships that wished to turn back—to wage war on Aros and retake Teyhalan land—they had reached the limit of their intentions. Those captains—and my father—had never actually looked beyond the horizon. They had always looked back toward the land. Something had been taken from them. And by abandoning my father's goals, I took even more from them. I took any hope of getting that land back."

Kadara knows well the draw of ownership. She could not imagine never returning to her cottage. She purses her lips and nods, cupping the glass in her hands.

Kala continues.

"They waited until I sent Rodahn to trade. He is the most capable fighter in Aros, and with me gone, he would be ruler and likely more pliable to the call of war. He is also a fiercely loyal brother. They kidnapped me in my sleep the very night he departed. I woke adrift in a small boat with no oars and with ocean meeting sky as far as I could see in every direction. My head pounded from the sleeping draught they had hidden in my wine. To kill me would have been too much for them. They abandoned me instead. Left me to the whims of an endless ocean." She smiles, seeing the look of concern on Kadara's face.

"I am sorry." Kadara touches her hand and nods for her to continue.

"There is no sadness in this tale, dragonslayer. I was born and raised on the sea. While they were all looking in toward the lost land, I was looking out, looking up. The stars are the same no matter what ship you stand on. They hadn't taken anything from me. I was exactly where I wanted to be. Further, I knew exactly where I was. I turned onto my stomach and paddled toward Aros.

"When Rodahn returned from his trip, he was told that I had drowned. That I had succumbed to the deep. He knew better, of course, and cut his way to the truth the best way he knew how. There was still blood on the surface when I came paddling up to where we'd last been anchored. Anchored in a murky pool of red water, the ship hadn't moved, customary during a period of mourning. Other ships had arrived, called by messenger bird to witness the ascension the newest ruler. For every ascendence, there is a ring made of the other ships, a shell around the pearl that carries the new ruler.

"When I arrived, there was no shell. All ships were pointed in my direction. Rodahn had given only one order: Find Kala. The sight of me, not only alive but coming toward the fleet, sent shivers through Teyhala. I had survived what some called death and others called a test from the sea. Loyalty among those conspirers not yet rooted out by Rodahn was immediately ensured. Pine as they might for the land, Teyhalans will always obey the sea. I am Admiral-Queen Kala of the Deep and none have been out as far as I have."

Kadara shakes herself free from the story's grasp, its lingering waves still beating against her mind.

"Thank you for sharing your story," she says in a heavy exhale.

"It is yours to tell," Kala says.

They clink glasses again, and Kadara shares her tale in full. She includes the truth of her amulet and the dragonstone blade. To omit from the tale, or to tell a lie, would be dishonorable. She could have chosen the story of her sword, or of a fine day at the market, but it would not have been payment enough for her rescue, or for the story Kala shared. Teyhalans trade stories with each other as sacred tender.

When Kadara finishes her tale, two bottles of wine stand empty. Kala thanks her for sharing her story.

"It is yours to tell," Kadara says with a clink of her glass.

Kala nods a solemn nod and calls for Rodahn. When he arrives, she recalls the tale as if the words were still flowing from Kadara's lips. Kadara watches the purple Ileri stone swing from Rodahn's neck in its slumber.

"The healer Isaleti gave it to me," Rodahn says when he notices. "She thinks me far stronger than I think myself. Perhaps she sees my destiny—"

"Or confuses him with me," Kala says, interjecting. "Either way, we have more pressing matters. A dragon to locate, for instance. We will send birds to the other ships and see who has seen what and where. You have an impossible contract to fulfill, Kadara." She looks at her brother. "Ro, can you convince Senni to change her command? I can't help feeling that if the death of this dragon is good for Drekan, it is bad for the rest of Aros."

"I will try," he says, "but she is a ravenous shark when the blood of someone she loves has met the water. That dragon took many a Naiwoan life that day as I recall."

"Send a messenger bird."

"Will we not sail past Naiwoa?" Kadara asks.

"Not yet, Dragonslayer. You are not the only castaway in need of rescue. We are on the way to aid another vessel along the shores of the western sea. Ro's reunion must wait."

Rodahn slips out of the captain's quarters with a nod. Kala and Kadara follow his boisterous laugh as he disappears above deck.

The crew hoists the anchor, and the ship heads west, a cloud of birds rising from its deck with messages for the fleet. Rodahn coos to one until the crowd disperses, then sets it free to the east. Before night falls, each of the messaging birds has returned with replies from the other ships and one from Senari. According to the messages, a blue sky dragon was seen near the Ayelomi, and Senari now orders Kadara to serve her twenty days working the Teyhalan way.

Kala orders the ship to set a course for the troubled sailors waiting in the western sea. As they pass the southwest corner of Alawhe Island, Kadara can see the sea lions crowding the low beach. She waves as they sail by, knowing they are happy to have their island back. She longs for her own island, the secluded holding atop the grassy hill, while adding another stop to her list of places to visit before she can return home.

J is for Journey. A voyage afloat. The waves hide such wonders just under the boat.

TEYHALAN SHIPS RESEMBLE WHAT KADARA IMAGINES THE MAINLAND OF AROS MUST LOOK LIKE WHEN VIEWED PEERING WESTWARD FROM BEYOND THE MOANAAKE ISLANDS. The aft rises in a gentle slope like the tree-covered Grovenkar Hills in the south. The fore is seated higher, evoking the towering Rockfell Peaks. Each sit well above the floodplains' deck and quarterdeck. The mainsail rises like Inati N'tan from a Sleeping Mountain deckhouse, the mast jutting straight up to meet the spread-winged sails that harness the wind like dragons.

As they make their way south, Kadara gets to know the crew of the ship. She visits often with the tailor, whom she comes to know as Wenna, to discuss string-making techniques and the proper oils for woven leather. Mornings are spent helping Rodahn train his men to defend themselves with swords, a practice Kala finds worthless. She steals Kadara away each day before noon to train her in navigating using a sextant and regale her with tales of the sea beyond sight of the shore.

The rest of her time Kadara spends helping the crew and pretending not to notice that the healer Isaleti is avoiding her. This she finds vexing, as she enjoys the company of wizards. The few who travel as healers aboard Teyhalan ships are renowned for their wisdom and abilities. She had hoped to share stories with one. When she mentions this to Rodahn, he laughs until tears are streaming from his amber eyes and drags her below decks like a smiling anchor.

Kadara has spent most of her time enjoying the brisk sea air. The darkness blinds her, making her rely on her enhanced senses to duck and avoid hitting her head on beams as they scurry past. Through the web of cabins, Rodahn pulls her until they arrive at a door that somehow looks older than the rest. He knocks, and a small voice calls out for them to enter. When the door opens, the sweet smell of smoldering herbs emerges, reminding Kadara of Jabo's cave and sending signals to her head and heart in concert. A plethora of lamps light the warm, smoky room, and Kadara is thankful for the ability to see again—all the more so when she sees who they have come to visit.

Isaleti Okun sits in a high-backed chair woven from the long, white reeds that line the shores of Beyekun Bay in the Moanaake Islands. Her gray canopy of hair is broader than it is long, reaching half an arm's length from her scalp in an even halo. Her wardrobe is the standard sailor attire, with the exception that her garments are more purple than any, aside from those of Kala. She smiles a warm, pursed-lipped smile and sets down a thick book without marking her page.

"I was beginning to think I had offended you, Dragonslayer," she says, motioning to a driftwood bench for her guests to sit on.

Rodahn waves her off, something the healer doesn't seem surprised by, and leans in the doorway looking uninterested. Kadara sits and apologizes for her absence.

"No, no, I am only teasing. It is much more fun up there in the sun, I know." Isaleti lights a pipe with a stem the length of her arm and blows the smoke out through her nose. Her golden eyes flicker over Kadara with a speed that only she can follow.

"Do you not—" Kadara starts.

"Go up there? No," Isaleti finishes for her. "Kala blames me for the things that break when I do that." Her eyes study Kadara again, as if scanning the page of a book she has read before. "You must be someone special to carry an Ileri stone."

Rodahn leans farther into the room, captured by the new subject matter.

"Each one has a different purpose, of course," Isaleti continues, "but each can only be given once."

Rodahn looks down at his new amulet and back at Isaleti. She winks at him and blows more smoke through her nose.

"No, I just found it somewhere," Kadara says, joking.

The healer laughs so hard that she coughs, and Rodahn shoots Kadara a disapproving glance. He rubs Isaleti's back and tries to take her pipe from her, but her frail hand grips it like a dragon's jaw, and he gives up after a while.

Kadara continues, "Orun Jabo gave it to me. It guides me to a dragon." She shifts on the bench, her discomfort rising. "Or maybe it was meant as a warning."

"Oh, that message was meant for you, dear," Isaleti says. "You won't have heard it wrong."

The ship lurches. "And that message is for you, dear." Isaleti points her pipe at Rodahn. He stands and shoots Kadara another disapproving glance before slipping through the door in search of answers.

"Have you enjoyed your time aboard?" The wizard's shifting attention falls back on Kadara.

"Teyhala is as welcoming and generous as ever. That, at least, has not changed."

"The sea doesn't change, nor do the stars," the healer says, "but what drives those of us stuck between them is as shapeless as water."

The ship lurches again, and Kadara stands to seek information.

Isaleti grabs her hand. "I need you to help me up the stairs, dear."

Kadara helps her to stand while secreting her pipe away from her. With the pipe placed on the dresser, she helps the healer toward the doorway.

"I thought you weren't allowed to leave your cave," she says.

"I'm allowed to do a lot of things when the ship is in trouble," the healer responds with a child-like honesty.

Kadara guides her to the stairs, bracing against the wall to avoid being thrown about when the ship heaves again. She makes certain that Isaleti is stable, then climbs the stairs. Better to determine the danger above than to lead the aging healer into it.

The hatch opening seems to rumble at her approach and Kadara has to push her shoulder into it to lift it. A mighty wind fights against her. As she prevails, sheets of rain lash at Kadara in horizontal ribbons, driving water into her ears and eyes. The crew are sprinting and sliding about the deck, yanking at ropes and bracing against the mast.

The ship leans hard to the side, and Kadara is thrown into the lip of the hatch, bruising her ribs. Isaleti pulls at her leg, and Kadara sinks back down the stairs, grimacing. The healer, her hair now tied back, touches her hand to Kadara's ribs for only a moment. Kadara feels a stinging cold, followed by a flush of warmth. When the hand is removed, Kadara feels no pain. She looks at the small wizard and offers her hand. Together, they breach the hatch and step into the storm.

Kadara keeps one arm around Isaleti to brace her and one in front of her eyes to block the constant onslaught of rain and wind. Through the storm, Kadara can see Kala calling out orders and cursing at the battering winds as if to frighten them back.

Isaleti nudges Kadara away by an arm's length. Kadara gives her two more, stepping farther away. Chuckling at the dragonslayer's prudence, Isaleti reaches her hands into the gale and turns them back and forth as if looking for something.

When she finds it, she clenches her powerful fists and rips them away from each other. The storm parts like curtains—but only for an instant. The wizard searches again.

This time, Kadara focuses as well. She listens to the space between Isaleti's hands and peers in like an eagle. When Isaleti grabs, Kadara can see small waves of air rippling in her tight grasp like fish pulled from a river. She yanks them apart again, and Kadara watches the storm tear like onion paper in the air and fold away like soft robes.

The wizard keeps her arms outstretched this time, holding off the power of the storm curtains. She lets them push in on her, their weight an unbearable crush, only to explode them back out with astonishing force. Her hair springs free of its binding as the storm clouds scatter from her center. Through the dispersing rain, the outline of a capsized ship looms, its sailors on a nearby island preparing rowboats. They wave and cheer, happy the requested aid has arrived. Isaleti is sweating and her breathing is labored, but she is not finished.

Kadara helps her to the side of the ship, where she can get a better look at the chaos left in the storm's wake. The overturned ship is undamaged, though its captain's ego may not be. With a large flourish that Kadara is certain is for show, Isaleti coaxes the wind to do her bidding again. This time, it returns the ship to its preferred position and dries its soggy sails for good measure.

The crews of both ships cheer, and Kadara joins in, clapping and laughing. She peers down at the rowboats leaving the small island. Though they have been stranded as Kadara was, they didn't build shelter or craft tools for hunting and gathering. They had no need for such things because they have what Kadara does not.

They have family who will come looking for them.

Kadara was on Alawhe for a year before she was rescued. It could have been forever. For the sailors of Teyhala, rescue is only a matter of waiting, and for a short time at that. It's good to be self-sufficient, Kadara acknowledges, but from time to time, it would be nice to know help is coming.

She can hear Rodahn coaxing the wizard back down the stairs. As she prepares to turn and assist, she sees a shipless shadow on the water overtake them. The dragonslayer pulls her sword and looks up. Rodahn calls out to her, seeing her alarm.

"What is it?" He looks up into the clear, empty sky.

"Nothing," Kadara says, shaking her head. She turns back, looking at where the shadow was and sees the water between the ships shimmer and erupt. Rowboats are thrown clear, sailors screaming and grasping for purchase.

Rodahn turns and bounds back up the stairs, his eyes gleaming like the spray of water around him. He draws his sword and calls to the wizard below.

"Stay out of sight. It may be a—"

The ship lurches again as if still caught in the storm, flinging those aboard sideways. The second ship, having regained its uprightness only moments ago, is still empty save for a few sailors. Kadara watches as the shadow blooms from beneath Kala's ship and heads straight for the rescued one as Rodahn reaches her side.

Those who have managed to reboard dive into the churning ocean as a dragon the color of storm-shadowed seas launches out of the water and through the ship. Its wings, having evolved to resemble strong, stout fins, cut through the hull and deck like water. Wood becomes projectiles, and sailors aboard Kala's ship dive or die when the wave of splinters and debris reaches them. Kadara slices through the wave in an arc large enough to shield Rodahn as well, hoping to give him time to reach the wizard. The wizard, emerging from the remains of the hold, has other plans.

The sea dragon lashes back and forth in the sinking remains of the destroyed ship, forcing sailors under and swallowing anything that glimmers. While it is distracted, Isaleti uses one hand to push the ship away on a gust of wind. With the other hand, she sends dragonfire sailing into the waters between Kala's ship and the remains of the other. She is just in time. The sea dragon dives like an enormous manta ray, leaving a patch of growing everfrost in its wake. The dragonfire collides with the wave of icy shards creeping toward the ship and bursts into a cloud of steam and salt water.

As Rodahn attempts to block Isaleti from its sight, the dragon reemerges and leaps into the air, launching everfrost at the wizard. She turns, pushing Rodahn aside, and sends dragonfire volleys to intercept it. As the fire makes contact, she uses both hands to push the ship as far from the dragon as she can.

Kala calls out for her crew to abandon the ship and storms below decks.

Birds flow out of the doorway, set free by their master. When she returns, she has a messenger bird in one hand and her trident in the other. She drives the three sharp points into the deck as the dragon rams the bow of the ship. When the dragon disappears beneath the waves for another attack, she whispers into the tiny bird's ear and tosses it high into the air.

Rowboats hit the water in a steady cadence. The dragon doubles back from beneath, attacking the escape vessels at random. Kala and Rodahn move along the side of the ship, wishing rowboat occupants luck and cutting the ropes that secure them. Kadara stays to help and joins them in forcing Isaleti onto the last rowboat with them. As they are preparing to cut away, the dragon drives its weight into the ship again, forcing it onto its side and sending the rowboat into the air. Isaleti pulls the wind around their boat and sets them down on the water as the dragon charges.

"I have one good push left in me," the wizard strains to say.

Kadara can see that Isaleti's frail arms are blackened with bruises from conjuring. She stands, running her hand along the edge of her blade.

"Then you'd best make it a big one, healer."

The sea dragon reaches striking distance, and Kadara winks at the old wizard. Isaleti stretches out her hands and nods. The dragon rears its strike, its eyes mad with fury.

"Now," Kadara says, and she leaps into the air.

Isaleti pushes with all her might, and Kadara is caught in the folds of the wind curtain. As the small rowboat is thrust away from the dragon, Kadara is catapulted toward it, her sword at the ready. She swings her trusted arc and prepares for the jarring jolt of contact that comes in the breath before whatever she presses her sword against gives way.

Had she been listening to the surrounding water, looking with her enhanced sight, feeling the temperature change in the air, perhaps she would have noticed the second sea dragon boiling below the surface. It cuts through water and air alike with a precision matching her sword.

Like the wind curtain beneath her, Kadara's attention is divided. The sword slips from her grasp as the seaweed-green dragon's jaw closes around her waist and pulls her into the murky sea. A bloom of everfrost spreads across the surface above them.

Kala calls out Kadara's name as the dragon goes down. Its companion follows. They will feast in the descending chaos, tearing chunks of flesh from drowned victims until the next unsuspecting meal floats by.

Kala and Rodahn look to the wizard for signs of hope. Isaleti's purse-lipped frown says all they need to hear. Kadara is gone. They row on to safety in silence, tears making small, salty seas at the base of every eye.

K is for Knowledge, the key to all doors. When you have it aplenty, you know you need more.

SEA DRAGONS. They always drown you first. Sky and cave dwellers get right to the business of disabling and devouring the meal. Rock dragons freeze their meals before digesting them. A struggling meal is not easy to swallow. Sea and river dragons are equally pragmatic. A drowned meal does not swim away.

All around her, Kadara sees the drowning, the surfacing, the panicked, and the dead. Whipfish glide through the water, scavenging. Parts of boats and bodies swirl in the churning of the dual dragons' dance. They are fearsome. They are relentless. They are living terror. A dome of everfrost begins to enclose their chaotic world.

Kadara reaches for her sword. She can feel it try to obey the order, caught in the pull of promised reunification once more. Something, though, is holding it back. She tugs again, and the ice above her cracks, reforming around the crack with equal speed. Her sword is stuck in the everfrost left in the dragons' wake.

She tries not to struggle. A struggling catch is not a drowned one. She calms her mind and lets her muscles relax. The dragon releases her and flashes toward the surface to bring down another rowboat. The force of its movement spins Kadara, and she yanks hard on her sword; the connection stops her turn and propels her toward the everfrost-encrusted surface. She releases the pull as an overturned rowboat comes crashing through.

The boat plummets toward the deep. Kadara cannot swim free fast enough and surfaces in the air pocket created by the hull. She fills her lungs with the life-saving air and kicks out from beneath the boat, escaping its downward drag. Pulling on the sword again, she scans the surrounding water. The sword is not moving. Worse, the everfrost has reached the seafloor and is closing in. A huge amber eye catches her upward momentum, and the sea dragon turns and charges her. She pulls harder at the sword, to no avail, and the dragon's jaw closes around her leg, dragging her into the darkness below.

***

"The smallest lights can only be seen in the deepest darkness," Jabo once said. Smoke trailed from an ember deep in the well of his pipe, and he was complaining about the weak light emanating from one of his lanterns. He fiddled with the ratchet and advanced far too much wick.

"It is very bright outside, Jabo." Kadara waited while her mentor unrolled a scroll and held it too close to the lantern. The soot blackened the rear of the scroll, and Jabo cursed at the tiny fire encased in the glass. "We could read out there. Sunlight is almost always bright enough. You could use more of it as well."

Jabo shot her an irritated glance and waved her off.

"That would defeat the point. Besides, we are not reading. I am." He fished a new lantern from a shelf and set about preparing the wick. "You are retrieving your sword from outside." He snapped his fingers, and the wick flared to life, its yellow light reflecting against his white, toothy grin. Kadara was not impressed.

"You always tell me to leave it outside."

"I do."

"You said it was the least useful weapon I have."

"It is."

"But you want me to bring it in."

"I want you to call it in, Kadara."

"Jabo"—Kadara pinched the bridge of her nose and exhaled a gentle draw of breath—"Jabo, I can't call the sword in here. I left it at the mouth of the cave."

"What if someone takes it?" A false panic rattled his voice.

"No one will take it, Jabo. I drove it so far into the stone that only my pull can release it. Even if they do, I can call it back."

"Then call it now." He lit another lantern and, satisfied with the glow of that one as well, set it next to the last and unrolled his scroll again.

Kadara turned and headed for the long, winding passage back to the mouth of the cave.

"No," Jabo said. "Call it from here."

"It is not a straight line, Jabo." She watched the wizard's head bob in agreement. "Okay." She took a deep breath and focused on her sword. She envisioned it there at the cave's entrance, buried in the stone so deep that only she could hope to remove it. She reached for it, and when she felt it in her grasp, she pulled as hard as she could. It was like holding the reins of a panicked horse. The force of the pull moved her instead, sending her flying into the shocked wizard's bookshelf.

"I said call it, not yank it! It's not a tooth, Kadara." Jabo rolled up the scroll again. This time, he waved her over to the table. A glass of water sitting nearby became his vehicle for explanation. "Hand me that," he said, pointing to another glass, one that Kadara had knocked from the shelf. She handed it to him, and he placed it on the table. With the scroll in one hand, he raised the filled glass and held it to the mouth of the scroll. The other end, he placed over the empty glass.

"There will always be the faster way to retrieve your sword, Kadara. The very direct way that goes from one place to the other unimpeded." He tipped the glass and poured the water through the scroll and into the other. "But you may not always have that option. I have taught you to use your other weapons first. Eventually, though, the use of your sword will be your only option, and there may not be a clear path to it. It is the same with the attraction to the dragonstone in your sword."

This time, he pinched the end of the scroll and poured the water in.

He waited while the water soaked into the thirsty parchment. When it was saturated, he unrolled the scroll. The water had been absorbed. "Though it may not be the fastest way."

Kadara watched as Orun Jabo squeezed the ink-blackened water from the scroll into the waiting glass. The lesson was absorbed: She remembered Ologun's instruction and waking with the sword. She hadn't pulled it at all, only summoned it. She flexed her hand and tried to call her sword.

"Sword," she said, "come to me." She waited. When nothing happened, she spoke louder. "Sword. Join me."

"Does it have good hearing?" Jabo asked in a loud whisper.

Kadara grumbled and closed her eyes. She thought about her sword, how the balance of the blade was perfect. She thought of the scar in her palm, how the sword fit in her hand like clay, how she didn't feel quite whole without it. She thought hard about the feeling of being whole.

Jabo's laughter and the weight of the hilt in her hand told her she was made whole again.

"Very good," Jabo said with a chuckle. "Now get that thing out of my home."

L is for Life, the first gift we receive. Both princess and pauper are born and bereaved.

The memory of Jabo's laughing jab echoes through Kadara's mind. She could never keep her sword in hand when visiting his hidden cave, but it never felt as far away as it does now. Kadara opens her eyes. She has had enough of dragons and water for a lifetime. The gigantic beast's fangs tighten around her leg, threatening to pierce the tightly woven sealskin, and she resists the urge to cry out and lose what precious air she has remaining. She stills her thoughts to still her body.

This time, instead of pulling at her sword, she calls to it.

She projects her thoughts as best she can, willing them to move through the cold water. Images of Ologun and Orun Jabo and home and being whole again flood her head until she can feel the hilt in her palm once more. When the dragon, believing her drowned, frees her to seek more prey, she takes its head and kicks hard for the surface. She breaches like a juvenile whale learning how long is too long to be under. With one hand locked around her sword, she treads water, using her other hand to guide her in a slow spin.

A glistening, blue sheen of everfrost coats the surface between her and the safety of the shore. The water below her warms in a deadly contrast, a stark warning. Before she can thrust her sword downward, she is taken under by the leg again. She thrashes at her captor, but the dragon is smart, and it is angry. It yanks her body back and forth, forcing her limbs into the path of her swinging blade.

Kadara goes still. She relaxes her muscles and closes her eyes, releasing her hold on the blade. The dragon adjusts its grip, biting down hard around her torso. Its fangs tear through the tough sealhide, puncturing her skin. She does not flinch. When the dragon releases her, she is lifeless, limp. Flotsam. The dragon is not convinced. It swims past her in violent arcs, flinging her body about with the wave of its movement. Still, Kadara shows no signs of life. Her lungs burn, and her bruised limbs want to stretch, but she is unmoving.

The waterborne beast is not persuaded. The sea dragon's enormous golden eye presses so close to her she fears her heartbeat might alter the pressure in the water enough for the dragon to perceive it.

A heartbeat is all she needs. In a heartbeat, Kadara can think of a thousand things that make her feel whole, and since she left home, she has added so many more. So many people and places that are now a large part of her. Stones that make up the mountain Kadara. In a heartbeat, the hilt of her sword is back in her hand, its blade buried in the giant, yellow eye.

The sea dragon flails in pain, creating a current of death and debris around it, but it is too late. Kadara spins, cutting the full way through the dragon, and surfaces for air covered in dragons' blood, seawater, and the remorse of having taken the life of yet another magnificent creature.

Dusk is falling. The water holds debris and bodies but nothing else. Hoping that more sailors survived than died, Kadara swims for the closest sizable piece of wood and hoists her body onto it.

A nearby set of barrels, with a length of rope still attached, floats close enough for her to reach them, and she rolls them onto the torn chunk of deck beneath her. In three swims, she pulls them under, one at a time, and fastens them to the underside of her makeshift boat at equal distances from the sides. Her raft stabilized, she pushes it through the water, kicking behind it and panting until she reaches another floating piece of deck. She lashes it to her raft and searches until she finds barrels to stabilize it.

A large piece of sail caught on some floating wood catches her eye. She maneuvers the raft toward it while keeping watch for more dragons and survivors. A patch of the sail remains above the water's surface, and Kadara holds it with a firm grip and carves a soggy square from the rest. Darkness encroaches as she works. From the side of her second piece of raft, she carves a large, flat oar. In and out of the debris field Kadara rows, collecting wood and cloth where she can.

At one stop, she finds the broken wooden bulb of Isaleti's pipe bobbing along and plucks it from the surface.

When she is satisfied with her scavenging, she hoists her sail on a makeshift post, stretching it to make a triangle with the far corners of the raft. She rests there, with the remains of chaos around her and her sail drying, until the wind can fill the sail again and the raft begins to move on its own. Once the sail has dried enough, the raft picks up speed. Using the oar as a rudder, she makes her way to the inky outline of the sandy dunes to the east.

The raft survives the journey, and Kadara disembarks on the sand at the edge of what must be the Solmar Desert. The sun-bleached bones of ships and sailors litter the narrow strip of saturated sand fed by the looming dunes behind it. She pulls the amulet from its custom-made pocket and holds it up in the moonlight. It is devoid of life; no glow emanates from the stone.

Kadara turns it again, rubbing its surface to be certain it is clean. Sniffing the air, she takes in the scents of the sea and sand and of several animals nearby. She can taste the salt in the air, hear the barking of seals along the shore. She listens to a rolling rumble approaching from the south and watches a pod of dolphins dancing in the distance. Her senses haven't dulled with the dimming of the Ileri stone's light. Still, losing its guidance concerns her. Kadara tucks away her amulet with Isaleti's pipe and climbs the nearest dune.

M is for Movement and shifts in the sands. You fall in the desert, you may never land.

SAND, AS FAR AS THE DARKNESS ALLOWS HER TO SEE, IN THREE DIRECTIONS. Water to the west. A patch of palms breaks the gray monochrome of the horizon to the east; a glimmer of what could mean hope flashes between them. It could be a pool of fresh water or the steel of a weapon. Either way, it sits in what would be shade come morning.

Kadara zigzags back down the face of the dune and drags the raft further onto shore as a tremor shakes the beach and sand cascades behind her, hiding the path she took. The sail's dingy white canvas is preferable to the woven black sealhide she still wears, but the material is thick. Kadara frees the canvas from the makeshift mast then cuts away strips from her sail parka, lessening the load and allowing more air to pass through. It would do nothing to impress the tailor Wenna, but it would serve as a garment nonetheless.

Satisfied with her defense from the promise of eventual sun and protected against the chill of night, she trudges back up the dune and sets a mental path in a straight line for the patch of trees. The sound of approaching animals grows closer. She can sense the weight and count of them now. The strikes of their paws against the warm sand indicate a long stride and heavy weight. She sniffs the air. Dried blood and wet fur tickle her nostrils. She is being stalked by two of the desert lions that roam the coast, searching for seals and shipwrecks. Somewhere south of them, an even larger beast continues to grow nearer.

This is Kadara's first time in the Solmar Desert, but her knowledge of its dangers is vast thanks to Jabo. She knows, for instance, that these lions will not stop hunting her unless they find something more appetizing. She knows, too, that they have a unique ability to sense the shifting dunes and avoid the desert's most dangerous predator: the sand itself. Haunted by constant tremors and always in motion like a giant, tidal ocean, the desert swallows anything at any time. To make matters worse, Kadara has become accustomed to the swaying of the ship after weeks at sea. It seems to have attached itself to her despite her arrival on semisolid land.

The sand is unsympathetic. Cavernous pits made invisible by a layer of grit open and close around the desert with no discernible pattern. The trees she is planning to walk to could be beneath a dune by the time she arrives or swallowed by a void below. Traveling during the day, when the lions are resting and burrowed, is not recommended. At night, one can follow the stars. At night, the sun does not press down like broken promises. At night, though, the lions hunt.

Kadara tosses her sword as far into the darkness as she can and drags it back. A long, intact line rests in the sand for only an instant. Thirty paces in front of her, the ground collapses, and the gaping mouth of a pit opens. She knows that—night or noon—she could not see to the bottom of the deathtrap. She waits for it to fill. When it has, she makes that spot her new temporary base, acting on the hope that a sinkhole will not open where one has just closed.

Along the vast desert she moves in her punctuated pattern, filled hole by filled hole. The lions keep pace with her, stalking along beyond her peripheral vision. Though she tries her best to hurry, it seems the oasis moves away from her as she goes. She presses on, chasing the horizon and chased by lions. Before long, the lions grow tired of waiting and prepare to attack.

Kadara turns her heightened senses toward them and freezes. They have become as still as the statues on Alawhe

Island, but they have not stopped for her. They are listening, she realizes. She, too, focuses her hearing. Though barely perceptible, even to her, the grains of sand are falling. Not only shifting and sliding but *falling* away from the surface. The sand, like captured rain escaping a sieve, is pulling away from the chilly night air all around her. Already, she has learned to sense the movement of the sands.

All around her, the sound of change rings out like a chorus of warnings. Kadara is so enraptured by the ebb and flow of the tidal sands that she does not hear the lions launch their attack.

Many types of dragons have charged her. She knows the distinct patterns of their attack, can often sense it before it comes. This is the first time she's been charged by desert lions. They do not move like any dragons she has ever fought. She prides herself on killing only when she needs to, yet these lions may make that difficult for her. They rush in at a staggered clip, each trying to drive her into the other. Running is not an option. Prey runs. She will not be prey today.

Kadara turns her sword so that the jagged point of her blade juts out from behind her elbow. With the hilt upside down in her hand, she presses the blade's sharp edge against her skin along the length of her arm. She has no interest in killing these beautiful animals. Digging in with her heels, she kicks sand behind her in constant heaves to create a screen and block the rear lion's vision. She parries and punches at the lion in front of her as it darts in and out, seeking a weakness. The sound of her own rhythmic panting disrupts Kadara's sense of the falling sands, and she steps into a half-filled pit as it closes. Her foot becomes sealed like an ant in tree sap.

The lions leap in unison as a tremor rolls beneath the desert. Kadara bends at the knees and falls hard onto her back, dodging the assault. Flipping her sword, she drives the blade beneath her foot and pulls hard, attracting the sword with the dragonstone in her palm. It works, wrenching her foot free from the sand. A pale glow from the east threatens to bring dawn into the arena, and the lions regroup for another assault.

The distant thrum from the south is getting closer, tugging at Kadara's senses. Still, she cannot make out what it is. The lions are far less concerned with what approaches than with their potential meal. They circle her, feigning and striking while forcing her toward opening pits, hoping she will become trapped again. Kadara, sensing the same, sways with the tide of their attack. They have chosen a hard target.

A fog rolls in from the shore, blanketing the dunes with a dewy mist as a new tremor shakes the desert. Dawn has arrived, and exhaustion pulls all three combatants into a dizzying spiral. When one lion tires of the dance and leaps at her, Kadara cuts an angled arc across the ground between them, spraying the beast with a wave of sand. Unable to see its mark, the lion turns in the air like a broken arrow. Kadara uses its weight and momentum to propel it farther down the dune.

Before she can regain her feet, the other lion strikes. Its weight hits her midsection. Still sore from the sea dragon's bite, Kadara absorbs the blow rather than deflecting it. She drops her sword to grip the lion's paws. Together, they roll until Kadara gets her feet between them and shoves the lion off her. They are halfway down the dune and still sliding as they stand, a river of sand following behind them.

The lion Kadara first sent down the slope sits crouched and waiting to pounce once she is within reach. Kadara yanks at her sword, forcing it to her through the mountain of grit, and stabs it into the sand, anchoring herself as the pursuing lion and cascading sand rush down around the waiting brute. Both lions are nearly buried. Kadara envisions them trapped, left to waste away in the desert winds, and action replaces thought.

She pulls her sword from the sand and charges down the dune toward the lions. She can hear a void opening beneath them. When she reaches the first lion, she leaps toward it, driving her sword far into the sand beneath it with the blade facing down.

The lion paws at her with anger as she moves on to the next. Buried headfirst, the second lion flails its back legs in panic. Kadara grabs both legs and lunges backward, pulling the lion free. Before the freed lion can resume its attack, she sprints back over to its trapped companion and leaps past it, pulling on her sword as she does. The freed lion sits and watches in confusion as Kadara leaps twice more, lifting the trapped lion higher each time. On the last pass, the lion leaps with her, shaking its sandy mane. The pit opens and swallows the deluge of sand that came down the dune but nothing more.

Kadara calls her sword and watches the lions. They check each other for wounds and then look back at her. When they both charge this time, she is too tired to put up a fight. She drops her sword and sits on the sand. The lions slow as they approach. They look at her with a primal focus, as if checking for wounds. Finding the torn skin at her midsection, one lion cleans it while the other cleans her face. Satisfied with their show of gratitude, the lions nudge her in farewell and bound off toward the coast.

Kadara convulses with laughter and falls back on the sand. The swaying sensation from the ship releases its hold and drifts into the ether. When she opens her eyes, her vision is filled with the stunned faces of the northbound Sharu'un caravan. They must have been watching her battle with the lions on their approach. She sits up and offers them her best impression of Torin's warm smile. A quake shakes the dunes.

"Am I trespassing?"

N is for Nomads. Always they roam. They need no
location; together is home.

THE SHARU'UN CARAVAN STRETCHES FAR INTO THE DISTANT SOUTH, EACH ENORMOUS, COVERED WAGON FOLLOWING CLOSELY BEHIND THE NEXT LIKE A LENGTHY PARADE OF ANTS HEADED TO AN APPLE LEFT TOO LONG ON THE GROUND. It grinds to a halt, the treads on its giant, armored wheels displacing the surrounding sand.

"No one owns the desert, sailor," a voice calls from somewhere in the sea of faces, "but you should probably not be here."

"I am no sailor," Kadara says. She kicks to the left, rolling away from an opening void with unnatural skill.

"No," another, smaller voice says, "that is not how they use their sails."

A pit rumbles open beneath the second wagon. The gaping hole swallows only sand, the caravan supporting each wagon with equal balance. The Sharu'un clearly created this caravan to navigate the dangers of the Solmar Desert.

"Come, lion tamer, we must leave this place." The third voice is authoritative.

Upon his command, the caravan grinds into motion. Kadara picks up her sword and jogs along beside the forward wagon until an arm reaches out and pulls her aboard. As her feet leave the sand, a large tremor shakes the desert. This one does not stop. It grows in force and violence.

The caravan rolls away at a steady pace as the whole of the dune, a section fifty times the voids Kadara has been evading, folds in on itself and falls away. Sand pours in from the surrounding desert, changing the landscape in its entirety. The dunes seem to slide about like sand on a beaten drum as the sun finishes mounting the patient horizon.

The caravan, Kadara finds, is designed much like a lengthy corridor. In a straight line, one could see from the lead wagon through to the last. The caravan never seems to journey in straight lines, though, instead weaving back and forth across the unpredictable sands. Each wagon is attached to the next with thick, woven bridges that stretch and contract with the movement of the caravan. Anchor ropes attached to the wagon tops provide the rigidity needed to support the moving structure over empty pits in the sand. Smells and sounds drift up from the rear wagons, teasing Kadara with the promise of musical and culinary delights.

The third voice speaks again.

"Welcome to the Shifting Citadel, stranger. You will not be needing your sword."

A tall, thin figure appears before her. He motions toward the treads of a large wheel, and Kadara sees they are made of steel. On closer inspection, she sees that the treads have hilts. They are swords, hundreds of them in each wheel. She waits while the wheel turns, sand falling away from the slow, churning blades. When a space presents itself, she sets her sword among the rest with a gentle chopping motion that sinks it into the wood without cutting through.

She turns back to her greeter. Where there was one, now stand three. "We are Flowing Sands. What should we call you, 'Lion Taming Not Sailor in Sealskins Who Dances with the Opening Void'?"

Kadara examines them, much as they do her. According to Jabo, "Flowing Sands" represents the fluid nature of rulership in the Sharu'un society. The title is not tied to one person but flows between three individuals who work-together, each embodying different facets of leadership. In any moment, any of them could be Flowing Sands, shifting without hesitation between the roles of leader, guide, and protector. This reinforces the Sharu'un belief that no single person holds power forever. Leadership, like the desert people, must adapt to survive.

"I am Kadara," she says. "Just Kadara." She considers herself and the sight she must present, wearing a tattered sail over punctured sealskins.

The tall, elegant man with the tanned skin and long, dark hair bows a slight bow and heads toward the rear wagons. Kadara's amulet lets her hear him speak to someone over the steady rumble of the caravan treads.

"Send word that Kadara lays down her weapon to help us carve the path ahead, and her strength becomes one with our journey."

He returns and continues the introductions, his robes flowing like the shifting sands. "I am Elihar," he says. "This is Shaja, and Kuguru." He nods to each of his counterparts as he speaks their names.

Kadara nods in response, but she listens to the rearward cars. Her name moves through the caravan like a steady wind, traveling the length and back again.

Elihar excuses himself, and when he comes back, he is smiling. "You have been accepted, Kadara."

Kuguru claps her hands and laughs. She has sharp brown eyes, made more piercing by the round, amber glass held in front of each by a rigid wire that encircles the glass and runs behind her ears. Her hair hides beneath a multitude of multicolored scarves that cascade like water down soft-skinned, brown cheeks made darker by the sun.

"Kadara, it is good to have you," she says. "I think you will find the Sharu'un far more hospitable than the naked desert."

"How did you get here?" Shaja has not stopped staring at Kadara's hands since she deposited her sword in the wheel. Her build is compact and strong, more wiry than muscular, with striking skin the color of shadowed red sand and piercing black eyes that absorb the details around her like water into sand. Kadara can make out light leather armor nearly hidden beneath her robes. She carries the only weapon that Kadara can see aside from those that have been given to aid in travel.

The weapon is a large, circular ring, carved with intricate swirling patterns that mimic the movement of sand in a storm. The outer blade is razor-sharp, while the inner edge is decorated with intricate golden engravings. The chakram has a metallic sheen, with colors that shift from gold to bronze, catching and reflecting the light like the desert sun. Kadara recognizes the craftsmanship. It is the Ologun Chakram.

"How is it you find yourself stranded in the Solmar Sea?" Shaja asks.

"A sea dragon attacked the ship I was aboard."

"Why were you on the ship?"

"I was traveling."

"To where?"

"To the southern seas."

"The Sharu'un will not be going there." With that, Shaja spins and heads down the long passageway connecting the wagons. The desert shakes with a fresh tremor.

"She likes you," Kuguru says. She pulls a small brass sextant from her robes and sighs. From another pocket, she produces a tiny vial of sand. She inspects the sand in the vial, shakes it, and returns it to her pocket. Stepping over to the front of the wagon, she peers through the sextant lens while pointing it at the dawn sun over the horizon. When she is satisfied, she turns to Elihar. "Thirty-six degrees to the right, north-northeast."

Elihar complies, turning a large, circular brass apparatus until the lead wagon is facing away from the shore. "Thank you." Elihar performs his signature half bow and sets a pendulum attached to the steering apparatus with brass pins before leaving.

"He likes you too," Kuguru says to Kadara. "He just can't show favoritism." She approaches at a gentle speed, adjusting her eyewear. "You knew that hole was opening beneath you.

You knew, like the lions know. Is that why they did not kill you? Were you raised by the lions?"

Kadara chuckles at the notion.

"I wasn't raised at all, Kuguru," she says, and Kuguru chuckles this time. "The lions are like any other animal—far more intelligent than most humans. Survival, respect, gratitude—none is worth much alone. They could have continued the fight; instead, they gained a new ally. Besides, an easier meal will come."

"I think, perhaps, I like you as well, Kadara. Please, call me Ku." Kuguru walks in a circle around her new friend, inspecting her disheveled clothing. "Come," she says, "let me guide you to some more fitting attire."

They exit the lead wagon as the path it is weaving through the sands turns back on itself. Down the corridor they stride, passing giant cogs and wheels, all turning or being turned by someone. Every tenth wagon seems to be dedicated to the forward momentum of the caravan. On either side are what looks to Kadara like the metal skeletons of headless horses; these are being straddled by workers who pump their legs in a circular motion, turning cranks with paddles attached to their feet. In response to the workers' effort, wheels fixed in place where the horses' legs should be spin like whirlpools.

One worker waves to Kadara and mops her brow before focusing on pumping in rhythm with the other workers.

Kadara waves back. She feels a part of the whole almost at once, accepted and welcomed by everyone she sees. In the momentum wagons, everyone seems happy to be at work, doing their part, moving things along. The chains and ropes in constant motion fascinate Kadara, and she watches and listens as much as she can until catching up with Kuguru becomes uncertain. When she does follow, she finds Kuguru waiting at the next wagon crossing.

"There is only one road in Sharu'un." Kuguru hops onto the next gigantic wagon. "But it is a road of wonders."

The desert shakes, and Kadara hops after Kuguru. Scents of desert delicacies make her stomach grumble as they enter a place Kuguru calls First Market. The exuberant navigator pulls Kadara along, into a stall full of lightweight materials that glide across her skin, offered in a spectrum of bright colors. Kadara insists on a modest, sand-colored set of robes. She changes into her new attire, careful to tuck away her amulet and the remains of Isaleti's pipe, and offers her sealskin in trade.

The merchant is delighted. He showers Kadara with more scarves and robes than she can carry alone, and Kuguru makes a humorous show of refusing to help. Kadara waves her off and attempts to carry the lot by herself, managing thirty paces before falling over. When at last they wrangle the bundle into two manageable boxes and head to the food stalls, Kadara is sore from laughing.

Elihar arrives to offer disapproving stares to the two new friends and apologies to the stall owners.

"This type of behavior is best in Fourth Market, I think," he says before leaving to manage some other seriousness in the leading wagons.

As soon as he is out of sight, the surrounding stall owners each shoot Kadara an approving smile or encouraging wave. She smiles back, glowing in the warmth. It feels good to be among kind people, and Kuguru seems like the younger sister Kadara never had.

They eat a meal of spiced milk, dried dates, and flatbreads coated in a variety of pastes, ranging from sweet to far too spicy, while sharing tales with one another. When Kadara finishes telling of her encounter with the lions, she learns that Kuguru was once chased by one. Kadara remarks on the similarity between the Sharu'un and Teyhalan customs, and Kuguru nods.

"We are all adrift. We simply travel separate seas. Even our methods of navigation are similar. This is the way with all people." She interlocks her fingers as she speaks. "Small knots along disparate ropes seem like similarities. They are identical upon closer inspection. These knots were tied by Aros long ago and will remain no matter how far we as a people unravel." She separates her hands for effect. "Like Teyhala, we prefer to trade and travel. Even without war and dragons, the people of Aros would have spread far from the Mother's Womb. We would never have remained the same. Aros, I think, is better, *richer* for it."

"You speak like a woman twice your age, Ku."

"Because I was taught by women twice yours."

They laugh and thank the merchants again before heading back toward the sleeping cabins. Along the way, Kuguru does her best to list the different types of wagons in the caravan. "Many are, as you saw, dedicated to locomotion. The riders are plentiful, but the task is tiresome. Having more riders means easier travel." She continues, "There are three libraries in the Shifting Citadel caravan, nine markets, seven classrooms, two forges, a construction wagon, and even a wagon dedicated to training. There are currently one hundred forty-seven wagons, though I could not tell you the uses for them all."

She ducks into the side hall of the sleeping cabins and points at the row of doors with beds painted on their surfaces. "Some are more obvious than others."

Kuguru leads Kadara to her cabin and points to an empty bunk. "It is yours if you wish. My past roommates have entered romantic relationships and taken up in wagons farther down the road."

One at a time, Kuguru unwinds the long scarves from her head. When the last is unraveled, her long, black hair tumbles down around her shoulders. She contains it in a braid and rolls each scarf before setting it on a tall wooden dresser. Beside the pile of scarves is the sextant and a small, yellow Ileri stone. It lies dormant.

Kuguru turns and says, "It was nice getting to know you today, Kadara."

"Likewise, Ku," Kadara says, placing a box of her new garments beside the offered bed. "I look forward to more."

"As do I." Kuguru dims the lantern attached to the wall as a rumble rolls through the desert. "I spend my mornings confirming and correcting our course. This is my calling. It is my contribution to the Sharu'un. All who travel with the Shifting Citadel must contribute. Do you understand?"

"I do," Kadara says. She is accustomed to doing her part at the market, preparing the stall for the day and securing it after the apples have been sold. "And I am happy to do my part."

"I am glad to hear it, Kadara. I truly am. I guide our people by following my heart, and today, it led me to you. In the morning, Shaja will come to collect you. She will help you find your calling as she does with all who come to us. Her calling is to protect the Sharu'un. Perhaps she will find you something of equal use. Perhaps I found you for some other reason." Kuguru bids her new roommate good night, and they fall asleep to the rhythmic sway of the caravan and the periodic rumble of the desert sands.

O is for Ojiji laying in wait. What some may call legend to others is fate.

KADARA DREAMS OF JABO. Not Jabo of the past but of a separate, impossible present. In the dream, he pushes the wind around them until they are lifted high into the sky like the glorious, cloud-residing dragons that first burst forth from the crust of Aros and never cared to touch the ground. Long strands of frayed rope connect every nation in Aros except Vulkanar, where all ends burn in a bright red fire. Jabo tries to explain what they're seeing, but the blue dragon attacks and swallows Jabo whole. Kadara cannot fight back. She cannot free Jabo.

She wakes and opens her tear-filled eyes in the darkness. The rocking of the wagon offers to lull her back to sleep, but she refuses its proposal and sits up in her cot instead. A soft, orange light flickers on as she rubs her eyes. Kuguru smiles at

Kadara from across the room. The reflection of the lantern makes tiny fires in the glass rounds she wears over her eyes.

"I'm sorry if I woke you," Kadara says.

"No, no. I am usually awake early enough to watch the sun rise over the dunes." Kuguru stands, and Kadara sees she is already clothed, having dressed in the dark. "I feared I had woken *you*, in fact."

She walks to the doorway and looks back at Kadara in the dim light. "You are welcome to join me if you wish. Shaja will find us when she is ready for you."

Kadara nods and dresses in one of her new robes. She leaves her dormant amulet on the dresser, confident it will remain there unharmed. She hasn't felt its warmth since she entered the desert and she will not have much use for the enhanced senses in so secure a place. She is drifting, she knows into a new life, away from her purpose. Still, her hand lingers only a moment on the amulet before she turns to face Kuguru. The smile, even visible in the dim lantern light, puts Kadara at ease.

Together, the two take the short walk to the lead wagon and climb to the top of it for the best view. As the wagon crests a dune, Kadara looks back over the caravan. It coils off into the distance, marking a stark line over and through the shifting landscape. The wagons look like a lumbering herd, teetering back and forth in a plethora of shapes and sizes.

On the horizon in front of them, the lantern of day comes unshielded from the wind of night and sunlight spreads across the sand like spilled wine. The shadows of the dunes dance about in the tremors of the morning. Kuguru stands with her arms spread and calls a Sharu'un greeting to the day. The desert answers with a low rumble. When she finishes, she turns to Kadara.

"Did you dream last night?"

"I did," Kadara says, recalling the sadness it brought her.

"Good." Kuguru does not seem to notice the melancholy enveloping her new friend. "Dreams are like stars that only we can see. If we let them, they will guide us. I dreamt well last night." She smiles, closes her eyes, and turns her face to the rising sun.

"And what did you learn, Kuguru?" Elihar peers over the top of the wooden ladder.

"That, as always, our course must change, brother. Sixty-eight degrees right. Sunni Ojiji does not sleep well this day."

Elihar sinks below the line of sight, and moments later, the lead wagon turns to the right and begins to weave its way south. The rest of the caravan follows.

Soon, Shaja's simple, white headscarf rises into view. She points to Kadara, then points down below the wagon's covering.

Kadara says goodbye to Kuguru and follows the protector of the Sharu'un down the ladder. When Shaja reaches the bottom, she continues down the long, winding corridor connecting the wagons. She does not speak, nor does she answer questions or look back to make certain Kadara is still following.

They walk as if attempting to reach the edge of the world and then they walk some more. While passing a storage house for grains, Kadara senses the caravan turning and hears others state they are headed east again. She greets everyone she can and finds that most already know her name. She tries her best to learn their names in return, but Shaja won't slow down enough to allow it. When they pass the wheeled wagons beyond what Kadara thinks could be Eighth or Ninth Market, Shaja stops and lets Kadara catch up. She leans against a closed door and speaks in a hush.

"Beyond this door lies the final wagon. There is always a final wagon, empty, waiting. The last wagon is a promise of growth, a promise that the Sharu'un will always thrive. When we are too many for the wagons we have, we will build another, and another, and another."

She opens the door and steps into the empty wagon. "Every wagon matters, you see? This one does not steer the caravan or house the grains or turn the wheels. It is not a market or a school. No one sleeps here. This wagon adds weight to the caravan that the riders must contend with. It adds length that Ku must calculate around. It is, however, no less important than the lead wagon. Both provide us with the same amount of hope, and hope will be our strength at the awakening of Sunni Ojiji."

"I have heard that name twice now," Kadara says. "Who is it?"

"Not *who* but *what*, and for most of us, *why*. As you know, we all serve a purpose. Mine is to rise before the dawn each day and train until I can hold off sleep no more."

"You protect the caravan."

"No. The caravan needs no protection. The Sharu'un have no borders to defend. There are no dragons in the Solmar Sea, and the lions never try to board." She chuckles. "Save for the one that chased Ku. Drekan of Vulkanar used to send his red-faced assassins and spies from time to time. Their weapons are treads on our wheels today. I do not protect; I prepare."

She sends the chakram whirling out through an opening in the back of the rear wagon. It flies in a perfect arc, adjusted for the movement of the caravan, and returns to her hand. "Just as the responsibilities of navigation and diplomacy are passed down and taught to those who have the calling, for generations the Sharu'un have trained warriors. Each day I train, and soon another like me will be born, and I will train them. Sunni Ojiji is why."

A rumble shakes the desert as if in response.

"Sunni Ojiji, the Great Dragon at Rest, will rise one day and devour the desert as it does." She sends her chakram on another arc and catches it as Kadara considers what she is hearing.

"A dragon? In the desert?"

"Beneath it. Sleeping since the First Battle called forth the dawn of dragons four hundred years ago. Inati N'tan was the first dragon, but many have followed him." She heaves the chakram harder. "Magic followed them." Harder. "And more war followed the magic." She slams the impressive halo into the wooden frame, sending splinters into the air. Kadara feels her amulet-driven senses bristle. "It is said that after Inati N'tan led the dragons to Aros, he dove back into the Sleeping Mountain. Sunni Ojiji, who was giving chase, faltered and landed in the Solmar sands. When man's desire for war destroys even the magic, Sunni will rise to finish what was started all those years ago." Shaja yanks the chakram from the wood as a new quake shakes the desert. "And the Sharu'un will stop it."

"And so, everyone has a calling. Everyone must contribute," Kadara says. She can hear two people moving at a steady pace down the caravan toward them. Their footfalls are far too deliberate not to catch her attention. With their approach, her senses heighten.

"Correct. Everyone except for you, Kadara." Shaja's words break her focus.

"I don't understand."

"Neither do I. Let me be clear: You are most certainly welcome here. You just"—she hesitates—"you don't *belong* here." Shaja takes Kadara's hands in hers and looks hard at them. "Ever since I was a child, I have been able to sense a person's path by looking at their hands. I have never been mistaken. I can see the work to be done in an infant's hands and in those of the elderly. I once saw purpose in a lion's paw. When I look at your hands, I cannot see a path. Not one that serves the Sharu'un."

"Not directly, anyway." Elihar ducks into the wagon, Kuguru behind him.

"You cannot see a path for her because she is already walking one," Kuguru says. She holds Kadara's blue amulet high in the air. It turns with the sway of the wagon. When it faces east, it glows. "Navigating would be far easier if my Ileri stone did this."

Kadara's heart races. The amulet has awakened. The glow is not a strong one, so there is no immediate danger, but her path has been made clear once again.

Elihar looks at Kadara's stunned face and sighs. He places his hand on Kuguru's and lowers her arm with a gentle push.

"Kadara," he says, "I do not believe we have had a chance to share stories."

"Not the right ones, anyway." Kuguru says. Her beaming smile puts Kadara at ease. She tosses the amulet to Kadara, who catches it and places it back around her neck.

Shaja laughs, her eyes fixed on Kadara's hands in the blue light of the amulet.

"Dragonslayer," she says.

Kadara frowns and nods, hiding her hands from the protector's deft eyes. A destiny of death-dealing is not one she is comfortable with. She explains as much as, together, the four walk back to First Market and share long emotional stories, expensive tales worthy of friends. Among the Teyhalan and Sharu'un alike, the urge to travel is as great as the urge to carry stories. Stories are like ripe apples, brimming with sustenance. Unlike the apple, though, they cannot be devoured or lost or taken. They can be gathered, they can be protected, and they can be shared.

In between stories, the four discuss the best place for departure, agreeing on the east-most point before the next significant turn of the lead wagon. Kadara appreciates the careful consideration her friends give to her travels. Destinies are large and cumbersome, but their burden must be carried alone. Still, there in First Market, with the sounds and smells of the Shifting Citadel mingling with the tales told around the table, Kadara feels the load lighten some. When she sleeps that night, she is met by softer dreams.

The morning brings relief and renewed anxiety at once, like two eyes peering through the predawn darkness. Kuguru has already left to perform her morning ritual. Kadara leaves the lantern unlit and steps out into the morning air. The scent of the distant forest greets her, and she knows they grow nearer to the point of her departure. She makes her way to First Market and sits for a while enjoying the sights and smells and sounds, and thinking of home.

When she returns to the sleeping wagon, Elihar is waiting with a hefty waterskin and a pouch of dried dates, flatbread rounds, and a jar of olive paste. He bows a low bow, seeming to imbue the gesture with more respect than usual, and Kadara returns the gesture before he wishes her safe travels and turns to leave. She listens to his steady footsteps moving down the corridor.

"Send word that Kadara must carve a separate path," he says to someone, "but that we are stronger for having journeyed with her at our side." Her name travels the length of the caravan and back again.

Kadara can recognize the voices of Kuguru and Shaja approaching from the lead car. She sits and waits for them, the amulet's light waxing and waning with the dancing trail of the caravan. When they enter, Kadara stands and embraces them both. When she is done, Shaja presents her with a gift of the finest leather armor she has ever seen.

"It is based on my own design," Shaja says, modeling her armor, "and it will not snag on branches and limbs in the eastern forests." She leads Kadara to a large, reflective sheet of metal where she can see herself.

Kadara notices she has grown more muscular in her recent travels; her skin has been darkened by the desert sun. She exchanges her flowing robes for the sand-colored leather armor. It fits as if she had been measured for it.

"Thank you, Shaja. It is perfect."

"It is the least I could do." She turns Kadara to face her. "Drekan is no longer satiated by his oppressive war on the people of Aros. He intends to destroy all magic—the wizards and dragons too. If he believes you are connected to the sky dragon, he will use it to his advantage. Be careful, Kadara. Be safe."

Safe is a promise she cannot make. It never has been.

Kadara looks at her reflection again as Shaja departs. She turns her head in the dim light, tucking the amulet into the leather breastplate. Her hair is far grayer now. Ku washes and oils it, combing the coils in long strokes. The oils relax her hair so much that, even without the weight of the braids, it cascades down her back in a glistening, wavy waterfall. Once satisfied the hair is no longer "dying of thirst," Kuguru gathers bunches that are the thickness of her finger in each hand. With deft skill, she twists them into twenty thick ropes of shiny silver and black hair, then binds the ends with ribbons of leather. When there are no more twists to bind, she covers Kadara's head and hair in a lightweight green scarf and wraps her arms around her.

"I have not seen enough in my dreams to guide you back to us, Kadara, but I know I will see you again. Dreams do not lie. Not in the Solmar Desert." She wipes her tears and describes the terrain that Kadara will face while traveling east.

When it is time, Ku guides Kadara to the lead wagon and instructs Elihar to turn due south. Kadara gathers her water and provisions and steps to the edge of the wagon. When the southbound turn is completed, the caravan is halted, and Kadara disembarks.

She closes her eyes as the caravan rolls away. When she opens them again, her sword is in her hand, and the wagons have traveled over a distant dune and are disappearing like the tears falling from her chin onto the dry and thirsty sands. One could spend a lifetime in the Shifting Citadel caravan and not see all the wonders it hides. In mere days, Kadara has seen enough to wind a thick rope bridge between its people and her heart.

She turns, feeling the amulet warm and remembering the sensation of its guidance. She follows. The sand grows rocky and is soon replaced by a brief stretch of dry grassland. The grasses then give way to a steady, brush-filled rise. The hills beckon her forward with ever greener shrubbery and the smell of a not too distant rainfall.

The sun sinks in the desert behind her, and Kadara finds a welcoming copse of willful trees growing in the patchwork hills between the desert and the forest. A heavy loneliness fills her heart, and even her shadow seems to stretch away from her as the day wanes. She makes camp facing west, her sword in the ground and her back against a tree, and sleeps until dawn.

P is for Protection. Shelter and sword. An offer of either should not be ignored.

WHEN KADARA HAS HAD HER FILL OF DATES AND FLATBREAD WITH OLIVE PASTE FOR HER MORNING MEAL, SHE SWIGS A HEARTY GULP OF WATER FROM THE FLASK AND PULLS HER SWORD FROM THE GROUND. Behind her, the sun is rising, and with it, the sounds of the forest. She listens to the birds singing and the leaves rustling and wonders how a dragon can hide in the Grovenkar Hills. Kadara has taken contracts from the Ayelomi, but the work has always been at the edge of the forest, never inside it. The people of the forest are protective of the trees they live among. Some say the trees reciprocate.

Most Ayelomi people never venture past the trees, so most outsiders have never seen one. Some say the Ayelomi *are* the trees, but Kadara knows better. Trees do not pay contracts. The Ayelomi are forest dwellers, with a philosophy tied to growth, both in agriculture and in knowledge. They are known for their herbal medicines and their harmony with the natural world. The hill-ridden forest terrain makes them excellent climbers, with a tradition of building their homes in treetops. Most outsiders haven't seen one because most do not look up.

Here, Kadara is a long way from the treehouses of Canopy Keep. She does not hear people living in these trees. Something moves among them, though. Something spry. She can hear them—whatever they are—darting between the trees, chasing each other through the undergrowth, leaping through the canopy. They are too low for tree-dwellers. They also move too fast. If assassins have come for her, they will find a fight waiting for them.

Kadara spins and runs toward the forest line at full speed, her sword thrust out in front of her. The trees explode with life. Frantic birds take flight, spurred on by warning calls from small game. She stops at the edge of the woods and listens. There is no more movement. No one breathes. The amulet's blue light pushes into the trees, laying a soft glow across the moss-covered forest floor. Kadara watches with focused eyes, waiting. After a dozen heartbeats, she sees movement in the moss. The soft, green carpet sinks, the pressure too slight for the weight of a human.

She kneels, laying down her sword, and takes the pouch of rations from her belt. Humming, she tears a large piece of flatbread from the round and tosses it toward the compressed moss. The bread is set upon by a swarm of forest dragons, too distracted by the free meal to continue camouflaging themselves.

When Kadara stands, they scatter, tucking in their bat-like wings and shifting their scales to bend the light. She has heard of these scavengers, the length of full-grown beavers, referred to as tree dragons as well. She will need to stay aware of them or risk losing a limb.

Sniffing the air, she tries to catch their scent but only senses a coming storm, one from which she must find shelter. The thick canopy will not be enough. The amulet's light beckons her farther into the forest. As she walks, she takes off her scarf and ties it to the hilt of her sword. She wraps the scarf around her thigh with caution, keeping the sword's blade from slicing through her armor or the scarf securing it. With the warm earth tones of her skin and armor, she can almost blend into the surroundings. The tree dragons, though, have all disappeared. She can still hear them circling her with curiosity. She counts six that follow.

Already at risk of punishment for trespassing, Kadara does not chance felling a tree for protection without permission. Instead, she follows the light of the amulet while searching for a hollow big enough to shelter in. Sticks and branches nestled among the fallen limbs are gathered in hand, and before long, she is carrying enough wood to feed a fire throughout the night. The clouds approach from the east like a charging battalion, pushing the scent of rain ahead of them like the songs of war.

Kadara marches on, the tree dragons still watching from a distance. Cresting yet another rocky, tree-covered hill, she finds a small overhang of stone and exhales a long yawn of relief. This will be her camp. She unties the scarf from her thigh and wraps it back around her hair. Using her sword, she cuts and digs away at the space beneath the overhang until she has a suitable hollow. The chunks of stone are perfect for building a dam around her fire pit in case runoff from the rain threatens to encroach.

With a handful of the collected wood, she creates a windbreak on the outer ring of the shelter to keep the fire strong. When she is ready, she lights the fire and stacks the extra wood inside her small cave for later, then plunges her sword into the dirt and sits back against the stone to wait for the rain. As the wind picks up, small and large game alike seek shelter or withdraw to escape the storm. They move westward with the windblown leaves, often passing Kadara's cave without noticing her.

Each offers a known scent: Moose, Wolf, Hare. Still, she cannot catch the scent of the dragons. She wonders at the idea of smelling dragons. One could smell the magic a dragon produces, smell a dragon's breath and blood, but the dragon itself? Despite her newfound abilities, she does not yet know the scent of a dragon. The idea fades as most do when given time to think about many.

She warms what remains of Isaleti's pipe over the fire and breathes in the sweet scent of rekindled memories. Like scouts of the storm, the first raindrops fall from the clouds to land outside the cave's mouth. A breeze pushes past the blockade, and the fire dances. More drops follow as thunder booms, sounding the horn of approach. Lightning flashes, painting the forest in blinks of black silhouettes against a gray sheet of rain. This will be a proper storm.

From her rations pouch, Kadara pulls the remainder of her flatbread rounds and the small jar of olive paste. She scoops small portions of the spread with torn pieces of bread and smiles, satisfied with this simple act. Rain pounds the forest, splashing from the roof of her cave and running past the dam at the mouth of her hollow. The fire flickers, warm and dry, as the cold rain plummets outside.

Soon, Kadara can see the rain bouncing from an ankle's height above the ground in several different spots, tiny puddles forming around each untouched space. She chuckles and pulls a handful of sticks from the dry side of her blockade. Six soaking dragons slip past the barrier and cozy up to her fire, shedding their mantles of invisibility in favor of friendship. Kadara portions out the rest of her flatbread, and the seven friends sit and watch the rain fall until the fire dims and they all fall asleep.

When Kadara wakes, the ashes have grown cold. Outside her den, the rain clouds have lost their vigor, and the sun is peeking through the branches in search of puddles to dry. She sits up in slow, rolling movements so as not to frighten her bedmates, but they have dispersed. Their questions have been answered. She is a friend. They need not watch their limbs around her, just as her limbs are safe from them.

Kadara kicks dirt over the dormant ashes and strolls out to find a large enough beam of sunlight to warm her in the crisp morning. Breathing in a deep breath, she tucks Isaleti's pipe away and catches a taste of smoke in the air.

Q is for Quarry, the hunted, pursued. A predator hunts but not always for food.

KADARA SPINS IN A SLOW CIRCLE, LETTING HER ENHANCED SENSE OF SMELL GUIDE HER. When she stops, she is facing north, and the amulet is shining its brightest. Shrugging, she turns back to her makeshift den and collects her sword with a swift pull and a flick of her wrist.

As she travels, the scent of smoke sharpens and is joined by a heavy haze. Kadara realizes she is likely approaching an uncontained fire. Wildfire would be devastating to the Ayelomi.

An ember from a lightning strike, kept well-fed by fierce winds and set tumbling over dry undergrowth, could destroy a forest in no time at all. This danger is one of the reasons for the roaming scouts who patrol the North Grove;

it is why Kadara should have been approached by now. She quickens her pace. A raging dragon with a belly full of flames can also devastate a forest. A dragon would keep the Ayelomi scouts distracted as well.

The amulet shines on, guiding her north. Its warmth, though, does not rise to show proximity. If a sky dragon is in the forest, it is not the one she seeks. She sprints on, pressing forward through the brush.

Soon, the scent and sound of fleeing animals engulf her. Using the trees as blockers, Kadara dodges through the stampede, listening farther north as she goes. Fire, yes, raging fire and something else. She stops, her feet digging in to the soft moss beneath her. She does not run to a wildfire but to one set on purpose.

Mixed with the roaring flames and suffocating smoke ahead are the clash of swords, the scent of fighting. Battle has come to Grovenkar Hills. A specter of movement catches her eye, and she turns to look but sees nothing. She listens with intent and hears six small dragons rustling through the trees. Their motion, though, is headed toward the fighting. Kadara's feet are moving again before she tells them to.

"Wait," she says, but the dragons neither understand nor heed her calls. She increases her speed. These are strange dragons, tame. She may not catch up with her new friends, but she will not abandon them to fight alone.

The new leather armor moves and breathes with the fluidity of shifting sands. Kadara pours herself through the trees, gathering concern for the forest dragons with each step. She thanks Shaja for her gift in silence, thinking of how at home the Sharu'un protector would be here, sprinting through the trees with her. The thought is fleeting. Kadara pushes through a curtain of leaves and is standing on the battleground, sword in hand, before she intends to be.

She hears what she thinks are the dragons, but they are camouflaged and moving at speeds that challenge the wind. When a well-armored Vulkanar soldier is pulled screaming to the ground by invisible forces, two others descend on their fellow soldier and end his misery with quick blows. The dragons move on, and Kadara tries to follow. The thick smoke and walls of flame push her back, and she hopes the dragons will be fine until she can find them. It seems they will be.

As she turns to probe for a way around the fighting, an arrow sails past her head. She spins to see an archer in green scamper up a tree and into the canopy. Behind her, his arrow juts from the eye of an attacker whom Kadara was too distracted to hear coming. A silent thank you sent, and she is moving again, chiding herself. She has not followed friends to a fight; she has stumbled unprepared into the middle of a war.

Known for their resilience, the warriors of Vulkanar have a mythos centered on the destructive and life-giving power of the earth. They have mastered working with mined and hardened materials, producing renowned metalwork. Sworn knights of Vulkanar bear heavy and intimidating armor, with plating forged from volcanic stone and metal engraved with fire patterns. Their tabards and shields carry the emblem of High King Drekan of the Forge: an anvil surrounded by a ring of flames. Each soldier is a fortress, a walking, killing example of Vulkanar's might.

While most Vulkanar people are farmers, spending their days tilling the fertile volcanic soil, many are raised to protect that soil. They are taught from an early age that they alone are born from the soil, and that they alone will rule all of Aros one day. So it is that a Vulkanar soldier, when confronted with the sight of a knight not wearing Vulkanar armor, attacks without question.

Kadara's second attacker is a loud breather. She hears him above the din of the burning battle. She dispatches him with a downward blow to the collarbone and disappears into the smoke. Arrows rain down from the treetops, most landing on upturned shields. Kadara waits in hiding for the next volley, her patience a blanket of warmth and calm. When it comes, the Vulkanar soldiers turn their defense upward to deflect the arrows. Kadara glides through the shield-brandishing soldiers like light through trees, cutting them down before they can lower their shields in defense. She does not enjoy the killing. She would enjoy dying far less.

The soldiers are well trained. Splitting into pairs, they alternate between blocking arrows and charging at Kadara and the Ayelomi fighting from the ground. When Kadara injures one Vulkanar, the others dispatch him, cutting the dead weight without remorse. When the Ayelomi gain ground, Kadara learns how the fires started. Volleys of lava rain down around them. Archers fall from the trees, screaming in pain. Kadara rolls a dead Vulkanar on top of herself as another volley sears through the sky like dragonfire.

The dragons, Kadara sees from beneath her makeshift shield, are not harmed. She watches as they attack the catapult designed to destroy their home. As it topples, she pushes the burning body off her and gets to her feet.

Around her, more Ayelomi are joining the fight, axes and bows in hand. They charge the forest's attackers, singing songs of war that Kadara has never before heard. She joins the fray. On the opposite side of the smoky battlefield, High King Drekan of the Forge joins too.

His shield is his weapon. A casket-sized layering of metals and volcanic stone, he swings it with two hands and decimates swaths of fighters. Its surface is rough and dark, like cooled lava. Red-hot cracks run across its face, radiating a faint glow as if molten magma is still flowing within the stone. The shield's edges are lined with sharp volcanic steel, designed not only for defense but also to inflict damage.

If Ologun had a regret to speak of, it was this shield. He made it for an honorable person. People, however, are pliable, and though Drekan's physique had remained the same over the years, his heart had changed. It had twisted and warped. He was the Shield of Aros no more. He had become its bane. The more power he seized, the more it seized him.

Drekan moves across the battlefield with a muscular and rugged frame, forged during his youth spent working in the Vulkanar mines. His dark skin is painted red with a mud made from the volcanic sands around the Sleeping Mountain, and his silver hair is cropped short. His beard is thick and well-groomed, and his eyes burn with intense amber. He moves through the battle in dark armor constructed, like his shield, from volcanic rock and steel. Though bulky, it is crafted with intimidating Vulkanar artistry. The jagged edges and fire motifs resemble cooled lava flows, with glowing cracks running along his breastplate and gauntlets, giving him an almost elemental appearance.

Kadara cuts her way toward him, slipping in and out of sight, watching him fight and studying his feints. Years of fighting dragons have taught her that no two talons are the same. Drekan has a single talon, but he uses it with deadly precision.

Whereas a lighter, thinner shield than his would be best for deflecting blows, this one absorbs them, and it does so with stunning efficiency. The force of arrows and melee strikes sink into the shield like a tired head on hay, transferring their energy to the shield itself. Each blow increases the brightness within the cracks, like an ember being fed by a passing wind.

Kadara thinks of the gradual fire that builds in the bellies of angry dragons and increases the speed of her approach. As she nears, she sees he is waiting for her. She sidesteps the final knight between them, taking his head for good measure, and charges Drekan. He is far faster than expected, dodging her thrust and delivering a punishing blow to her back with the flat of his shield.

Kadara winces and stumbles but keeps her footing, surface roots and fallen knights threatening to upend her balance despite her quick feet. Drekan slams his fist into his shield, coaxing a slight increase in color, and gives her a confident smirk. He has fought in many battles. At times, victory has slipped from him, but his confidence never wanes. He is fed by an unnatural fire that burns outward through his amber eyes.

Kadara smiles back. She's never lacked fire. She steps in and tests his defense, listening to his heartbeat. Sending swings and thrusts beyond the edge of his shield range, she coaxes Drekan into relying too heavily on his feet. He dodges and steps with a nimbleness that denies the cumbersome armor, twisting with her rhythm to keep his shield on the attack side while avoiding her sword. The rhythm is the point, though. Not the blade.

She breaks from the pattern with a double step to the right and slices at his shoulder plate. Drekan swings the shield back in time, but it does not matter. The sword slices through shield and armor alike, cutting within a hair of his skin. His shoulder plate falls away, and Drekan steps back, confused, reassessing the threat before him. The shield glows like a sunset along its shorn edge. He stares at Kadara's sword. His smirk has faded.

Through each battle, an energy surges. One that, if visible and viewed from above, would appear as a chain of lightning connecting each fighter, merging their worlds into that of the battle. They would be connected not only by the heat of the conflict and the rhythm of the sparring but by the thin, vibrating edge the fighters stand upon. Here, there is no room for thought, no time for consideration. Here, experience outweighs speed, and determination overcomes strength. Here, the river of destiny splits, and the current is strong in both directions.

Kadara presses again, forcing Drekan to step and turn to avoid her blade, but he is as smart as he is fast. His breathing and heartbeat remain steady. He ignores her rhythm this time, focusing instead on her wrist while he moves across the forest floor. When she feints, he takes the opening, striking the flat of her blade to break her defense and bashing her in the chest with his shield. She staggers back, stabs her rear foot into the ground, and kicks forward into another press.

Kadara is smart as well. She twists her sword as she strikes this time, preventing Drekan from parrying the flat of her sword with confidence. With each attempt he is forced to withdraw his shield quickly or risk losing another piece of it. He changes tactics, pushing the fight into the cloud of battle to involve more knights. With a forest of fighters surrounding them, Kadara is forced to rein in her slashes and rely more on thrusts and stabs to avoid injuring her new allies. Drekan relishes the chaos, letting it feed his frenzy and his shield alike. He absorbs all the strikes he can, coaxing the nearby Ayelomi to attack him and dodging Kadara all the while.

Kadara's concern for her six small friends has not waned, and she finds herself hoping for an opening in the fighting soon. Yet with Ayelomi and Vulkanar lying like logs at their feet, she and her enemy continue dancing a duet among many. When the glow of Drekan's shield is nearing that of dragonfire embers, Kadara doubles her attacks in desperation. Drekan moves backward in quick steps, ducking and dodging. Unable to break his defense, Kadara yells in frustration and flings her sword at him.

He sidesteps it and turns back to Kadara with his customary smirk. She smirks back, her scarred hand stretched out toward him in waiting. She pulls hard, and her sword responds in kind. It cuts through the air toward her with such speed that the air itself screams in terror. Drekan, puzzled by the outstretched hand of his enemy, almost misses the sound, only hearing it at the last second.

He turns to investigate as the sword arrives, pulling away just enough so that the blade slices open the flesh beneath his right eye. Blood springs from his face, and his lungs erupt in a cry of anger and pain. Kadara prepares to press her advantage, and Drekan reveals his. He slams his shield down hard on its bottom edge. The thermal energy explodes outward, sending Kadara flying back into a tree and shattering her amulet, Isaleti's pipe, and anything else in the immediate path of Drekan's devastating attack.

The six dragons pounce. As Kadara loses consciousness, she sees a a larger swarm of tree dragons to join them in their attack on a retreating Drekan and his forces.

R is for Recovery, healing of mind. The body and soul
tend to follow in kind.

D**REAMS AREN'T TANGIBLE.** Worse, they are made of a special ether that, when left to spread like spilled water, will fill any space available. Uncorked, they disperse, fly free. The amulet acted as a repository for Kadara's dreams, allowing her to collect and catalog them. She knows this now.

It is a brand-new understanding, gifted to her by the dreamless darkness from which she now wakes. It is an understanding confirmed by the loss of her heightened senses, the lack of sounds and smells beyond her ordinary perception, and the aching in her heart. She can feel an excess of pain but knows it will fade as well. Anger, sadness, and longing linger. Sleep, however, does not.

She opens her eyes. She is no longer in the forest. Instead, like thirsty roots, she drinks in the sight of a sparse wooden room. She lies in an enormous bed; soft green leaves and giant, fragrant flower petals support and comfort her.

Above her, a lantern hangs from a beam. Thin wisps of smoke dance from the tip of the flame and escape the glass enclosure. Kadara can smell only the petals cradling her head.

She cannot smell the lantern. She cannot hear the subtle roar of the fire eating away at the wick. She cannot sense the warmth of the tiny flickering flame from so far away. Her amulet is gone, and with it, its spectrum of senses. She feels frightened and lost. She feels alone.

She is not alone.

"Found your way back, it seems." A soft voice emanates from the edge of the cozy bed. "A sleep that deep can be like a prison."

Kadara peers over and sees that the words trail from lips that dwarf the size of the mouth they frame, set below eyes that dwarf the size of the lips. Though the woman's enormous brown eyes crowd age from her facial features, they hold a wisdom gained only with a long and storied life on Aros.

The woman's hair falls across her shoulders in long, gray locks. Wooden arrowheads hang from the ends, affixed with thin coils of yellow metal. Kadara's gaze sinks to the woman's pendant. A green Ileri stone in teardrop form sleeps surrounded by a tiny wooden basket of carved branches. Kadara sheds a tear of longing and falls back asleep. Still no dreams come, only the darkness.

"Were they difficult dreams?" The woman asks when Kadara later awakens.

Her name is Orisunomi. She says she is named after the Orisunomi Lake, which, along with natural springs throughout the Grovenkar Hills, feeds the mighty Apori River. Her people call her Omi, which she prefers to her full title. Her husband, though, the people will always call Elder-King Igiwa the Verdant.

"Sadly, I wasn't dreaming," Kadara says. "Apples ripen on the branch, but storms choose when they fall."

"Why does that make you sad?" Omi is patient and calm.

"Dreams are important."

"Not always. I once dreamt of rock dragons made of steel sleeping on a faraway moon. That doesn't seem very important, does it?"

"It does, actually." As she speaks, Kadara is joined by a familiar friend beneath the blanket of silk and moss. The tree dragon nuzzles her chin and roots around in her bed for crumbs.

"Shoo!" Omi chases it to the door of the room, and it scampers away with a screech of insolence. As she turns back to Kadara, the door swings open behind her. She spins to admonish the dragon, but sighs a sigh of warm recognition instead. "Well, it's about time." She pushes into the hall, and she and another speak with hushed voices.

Kadara does not bother trying to listen, but her hand drifts toward her chest in search of the amulet's comforting warmth. Omi steps back into the room and offers Kadara a reassuring smile as the wind-wielding wizard from the forest battle steps into the wooden doorframe. "Kadara, this is my husband, Elder-King Igiwa the Verdant, the great wizard of the woods."

Igiwa has a tall, robust figure with a presence like a towering tree. His skin is dark and weathered, and the gray hair cascading from beneath his crown is in long and thick dreadlocks, "decorated" with leaves. His beard is equally admirable: a cloud of gray streaked with glints of silver and, judging by the odd movements it displays, likely hiding a squirrel. The lord of the Ayelomi's eyes are deep gold, reflecting the wisdom of the forest. He bears scars—surely from battles fought in defense of his kingdom—and still wears the armor he must have donned for the latest.

Like that of Drekan, Igiwa's armor is an organic fusion of nature and metal. The bark-like leather is dark brown, with vines and intricate leaf patterns etched into its surfaces. The metal elements resemble tree roots, winding across his chest and arms. His helmet is a crown with antler-like adornments, clearly symbolizing his deep bond with the forest. A bow-axe hybrid is slung across his back, ready for both ranged combat and close fighting.

"You knew Ologun?" The wizard leans through the half-open door, his crown struggling to fit inside the low frame of the doorway. "Forgive me. Doors should be shaped like the creatures who use them, don't you think?" He speaks at the slow speed of growth. "I see that you have met my wife, Elder-Queen Orisunomi the Fert—"

"Iggy, no." Omi sits beside their guest and glares at him. He clears his throat and finishes the arduous task of entering.

"Ologun was a friend." His voice is low and resonant, like the call of a giant owl. He pats his strange, hybrid weapon and chuckles.

Kadara looks around but does not see her sword.

"The Worldsunderer must remain . . . outdoors. Canopy Keep is a living stronghold. We must protect her. I am sure you understand."

Kadara does. A treetop fortress in the Grovenkar Hills, Canopy Keep blends into the forest. It is constructed of living trees and stone, emphasizing harmony with nature and hinting at the well-kept secret that its old and storied ruler, Igiwa the Verdant, is a wizard.

"Orun Jabo is also a friend," Igiwa continues. "He will be pleased to learn that his Ileri stone protected you."

"He will be disappointed that I allowed it to be destroyed." Kadara hangs her head. Omi wraps an arm around her and pours comfort into her soul with a smile.

"No," she says, lifting the green stone hanging from her neck. "He will be proud that you held it so close to your heart. A wizard can only create an Ileri stone once in their life. To entrust it to someone takes a great deal of faith and even more love." She looks at Igiwa.

Kadara watches the two of them, suddenly aware that she is an unannounced visitor in a private home. She stands with too much haste, and her head fills with fog. She sits back down, and Omi steadies her.

Kadara has been in Canopy Keep for the better part of four days now, she learns, recovering through bouts of sleep. She can't count herself among the lucky survivors of those who were in the path of Drekan's blast. She is the only survivor, from what Omi has told her.

The soldiers who witnessed the Vulkanar assault have also told Omi the tale of the resolute knight who locked steel with Drekan and held him long enough for aid to arrive. Omi recounts the tale of the razor-sharp sword and the strange blue light that burst forth as Drekan's shield exploded, protecting the knight from the destruction that befell those around and behind her.

"The stone saved your life, but just barely. You need to rest."

"It was guiding me." A tear forms in the corner of Kadara's eye and threatens to drag more with it when it goes over the edge.

Omi tightens her comforting embrace.

"You must trust that whatever path it painted for you will be marked on your life's canvas. For now, those signs wait in darkness. In time, the light will reveal the path again."

"This is the way for all people," Igiwa says, nodding. "Even Jabo required rest and patience while here."

Kadara rises from the bed again, pulled by some unknown force within her.

"Jabo was here?" She can feel Omi glaring at her husband again. "When?"

Omi stands and faces Kadara, a sigh heaving in her chest.

"It was a few days before the fighting began," she says. "Jabo was here for help in finding his own path. Wizards can live for quite some time, but eventually, age wears on them." She looks at Igiwa. "Sometimes it helps to be in the company of another wizard."

Kadara would kick herself if the pain weren't already unbearable. She had just missed him, just missed her answers.

"When word arrived that Drekan had learned of his location, he fled out of fear that he would bring violence to the Ayelomi," Igiwa says as Kadara's vision slowly darkens.

"Drekan would have come eventually, anyway," Omi says. "He aims to come for us all one day."

Kadara collapses, still weak from the blow taken in battle. Igiwa calls forth a gentle wind to settle her in the bed of leaves and petals. As Omi pulls the petal blanket over Kadara, a tree dragon sneaks beneath and nuzzles with her for warmth.

This time when Kadara sleeps, she dreams. It is only a small dream, a spark not near enough a candle to call it light, but any spark triggers hope in true darkness.

When she wakes, Igiwa has gone, and Omi waits with water and nuts to replenish her patient's health. She nurses Kadara in person, taking supplies from a caregiver who visits each day to offer updates on the other patients. She tells Kadara that she, too, considers Orun Jabo a friend and is happy to help anyone he loves. For her newest patient, Kadara notices, she even pretends not to see when there are sneaky little visitors.

Once Kadara is able to sit up again in the bed, she enjoys the company of her maternal host.

"Are you a wizard too?"

The question makes Omi chuckle.

"No, dear, I was born to humans in the Southern Thicket, where the cliffs rival the steepness of Drakhaalan towers."

She sits down on the bed, and Kadara hides her grin. The chance to tell a story seems to be the perfect trap for Orisunomi. Words flow from her like the waters of the Apori River. "The woods were wilder back then. Not just the animals were wilder, but the dragons and the people were too."

A tree dragon darts into the room, oblivious to Omi's presence. It leaps onto the bed and slips beneath the soft petals. Omi chuckles and shakes her head before continuing her story. "The Ayelomi had no leader. As I grew older, so did my desire to change that. My claim was, of course, challenged. From the Northern Grove to the southern seas, I felled challengers like diseased trees until there was one remaining: Jin Igiwa." Her smile is radiant.

"He agreed to meet me near Orisunomi Lake to settle it once and for all. I arrived first, my witnesses at my side, and waited for him, ankle deep in the fresh mud, the giant seedpods of the alado tree floating around me."

The dragon peeks its head out from the bedding and darts back in with a loud chitter when it sees Omi. Kadara shushes it and nods to Omi to continue.

"Iggy arrived with no retinue, no witnesses, no weapons," Omi says. "A river of creatures stretched behind him and bowed with him when he reached the edge of the lake. I waited for him to state his claim, certain that I would do battle with a wizard that day." She shakes her head. "Jin Igiwa brought no claim to the throne. Instead, he brought an offer of peace: the loyalty of every animal in the Grovenkar Hills. He said that, in my spirit, he had found the one true treasure in all the forest. With one look into his eyes, I found it too."

When she glances up, Kadara is clutching her heart and swaying back and forth. Omi stands to leave in mock fury. Kadara, satisfied that her jab has landed, laughs and gestures to Omi.

"Okay, okay. Go on."

She does.

"I have known a few wizards—friends of Iggy's—and all have been equally kind, but none have eyes like Jin Igiwa. I fell in love standing on that muddy bank, and Ayelomi has been at peace ever since. Now, Drekan threatens all of that and more. But enough of romance and war. You need more sleep."

Kadara obeys her doctor and friend and rests while seeking dreams. They continue to evade her.

When she is strong enough to leave the bed, she makes her way to the door. Beyond it, she sees a steady stream of injured fighters being brought in for care. Elder-King Igiwa the Verdant blows through like a mad wind, healing those he can and offering words of encouragement to those he cannot.

Her tiny bedmate barks a small goodbye and follows its ruler to join the fighting.

S is for Strength, both without and within. The war with oneself can be hardest to win.

VULKANAR CONTINUES THE FIGHTING IN THE FOREST, SPREADING THE AYELOMI THIN IN AN EFFORT TO OVERWHELM THEM. Igiwa is indomitable, but he cannot be everywhere at once, least of all at Canopy Keep, where his guest has begun to feel the urge to join the fight.

Canopy Keep, Kadara comes to learn, is shaped in the almost-round form of tree trunks. A long, winding corridor along the outside of the stronghold connects to every hall. It allows light to filter through its windows and into the deepest rooms at the center of the massive tree fortress.

Kadara runs along this corridor daily, stopping often at the northernmost windows to see the smoke rising from the forest. When the frustration at her injured state reaches its peak, she runs the length of the corridor again. If she cannot feel the outer world, she will feel her lungs burn and her muscles ache. Omi is patient, as always.

"There comes a point where you do more harm than good," she says one day, leaning against the northern windows as Kadara approaches on her run. She hands her a much-appreciated skin of water.

"It's time," Kadara says. She points toward the north with her chin and drinks the water.

"It is not." Omi takes the empty skin from her.

"You are patient to a fault, Omi. I do no one any good running in hallways. Your people need my sword."

"If that were true, we would have it." Omi points to the far delineation between forest and plains. "Do you see the tree line?"

Kadara nods.

"When the tree line moves, I will be concerned. Until then, there are just fools being rude in the forest. The Ayelomi can handle it. You still have healing to do."

"I am as strong as someone half our age."

"Not all healing relates to the body, Kadara, and not all the healing we do relates to ourselves. You need to take the time to let your loved ones know you are well. Then take time," she says, walking away, "to convince yourself." She rounds the bend of the hall, still calling out to her impatient guest. "Maybe then I'll believe you."

In the morning, Kadara enters the treetop rookery draped in a weave of guilt and purpose. She sends messenger birds to Flowing Sands, Kala, Torin, and Senari with small side notes in Kala's and Senari's messages for Rodahn, wherever he may be. She chides herself for forgetting one of Jabo's most important lessons. He does not keep or accept birds, or she would have sent several by now.

Her daily runs turn into thoughtful strolls. Disencumbered by the weight of heavy breathing and the burning of her muscles, she can feel other things again. Somewhere, hidden beneath the blanket of longing for her amulet, a longing for companionship keeps peeking out.

The world she used to know is the world Drekan still lives in. One of constant strife and bloodshed and loss. Solitude was not only defensive; it was also forced. Other, like-minded people chose isolation to shield themselves from potential treachery as well. It was a world full of dragon hunters, glory hounds, and war. Somewhere around the time she became a recognizable face at her local market, the world changed.

Teyhala is now trading with nations that once sought to destroy it, and the crown prince of Teyhala is in love with to the queen of Naiwoa. Across Aros, dragons still roam, and rulers still pass judgment, but war is no longer the guiding principle. Not unless Drekan is involved.

Kadara comes to recognize that while the amulet had given her enhanced senses, it also dampened other feelings. Without the distraction of sensing everything around her, she is confronted by the feelings within. She understands, at last, that though she came to know many people in her past travels and learned of many lands in her studies, she never made any genuine friends other than Ologun and Orun Jabo. Jabo's cave and her holding were the only two places where she ever felt comfortable enough to close her eyes for more than a blink. Now, she has what Omi calls "loved ones." When Omi told her to contact them, it took Kadara no time at all to identify the people who fit that definition.

She loves Ologun, though he's gone, for the path he cut for her. She loves Orun Jabo for the guidance he provided along that path. She loves her new friends for the purpose they have added to her path and for the many new places they've shared, where she can feel safe, awake or asleep.

Before leaving the long, wooden lofts built to house the Ayelomi messenger birds, Kadara writes two more notes, one for each of her gracious hosts. She tucks them both beneath the door to Omi's workshop on her way back to the guest quarters.

Unburdened and feeling lighter on her feet, Kadara strolls down the corridor. For the first time, she notices the cool, constant breeze that runs through the hall. She smells hints of smoke in the air but also the fragrant alado flowers that bloom in the Grovenkar canopy. In the air, she can hear the far-off roar of the Apori River and the occasional shout carried on the wind.

She can feel the pull of her sword. It is a gentle tug at her palm. She explores this feeling that has been with her for so long. This sense is one of her oldest memories, ingrained like the scar in her palm. It is forward now, present. For so long, she acknowledged it like her nose, obvious and disregarded at once. Now, without the mask of the Ileri stone's light, the call of her sword is once again the strongest thing she senses.

That, and something larger, farther away. She shifts her focus to it. Like trying to peer into a fog or listen for her name in a crowd, she aims her palm and tries to concentrate her focus as small as possible. Her arm drops; beads of sweat roll down her forehead. She staggers back to the bed and lets sleep take her again.

For days, she stands at the north window and focuses. Each time, she shrinks the zone of focus. North becomes "just so many days north," which turns into "north-north-east" and pulls west at one point. Kadara realizes she is tracking the dragon. The shard of her sword, its essence now coursing through the dragon's veins, is calling to her.

She takes off running again, this time not for pain or self-punishment but for joy. She runs down the entire corridor and stops at the north window again. She can sense her sword below her, in the forest. She can sense the fighting. Omi joins her.

"I can sense the dragon," Kadara says. "I can *find* it." She turns to Omi, who is smiling.

"I believe you." From her satchel, she produces a packet of small letters. She hands them to Kadara. "You have correspondence. Once you have had time to read them, please join Iggy and me in the dining hall." She gives Kadara's hand a warm squeeze and glides off down the corridor.

Kadara looks at the letters in her hand and feels herself smiling a toothy, Jabo-like smile. All her friends have written back, including Omi and Igiwa.

In her hand, she holds proof that Aros has changed, and that she has changed as well. She presses the letters against her heart and returns to the guest quarters. Once alone and hidden behind the large, wooden door, she opens each letter, smoothing its folds with reverence, and sets them in an arc in front of her. One by one, she reads the responses, laughing and blinking away tears of joy to hear that her friends, her loved ones, are safe and happy.

Omi's letter is filled with the encouraging words of a proud friend.

Torin sends word that a Lorgan Dei tournament will be played with or without her, but he hopes it will be with her. He asks that she return through the gates, as children have begun to peer through the keyhole into the Greyhaal labyrinth again. The appearance of a dragonslayer behind the door would no doubt give them too large a fright.

Kala has drawn up new ship designs based on the encounter with the dual sea dragons. She insists that Kadara be present for the maiden voyage of the prototype ship. Isaleti sends her regards as well. She is carving a new pipe.

The letter from Senari is folded around the letter from Rodahn like a lover's embrace, and they each speak about the other more than themselves. They plan to wed. A true joining of the kingdoms. They both insist on her presence once they agree on the day.

The three letters from the desert are all signed Flowing Sands, but Kadara can tell the differences between them. Not only in the manner of the writing but in the words as well. When read together, they tell her that, like the caravan, some souls must stay in motion for what is coming. They say that when she rejoins the caravan one day, its people will greet her with open arms. Her overabundance of scarves is waiting.

Igiwa's letter is the shortest, but it is no less impactful. In it, he bestows upon Kadara a permanent guest chamber in Canopy Keep, one for her to visit and stay in whenever she chooses (given that she leaves the Worldsunderer outdoors).

Kadara binds the packet of letters in slow, deliberate motions. They offer as much guidance as her amulet once did and as much comfort as well. She sets them at the end of what is now her bed and composes herself for the walk to the dining hall. The walk is short, but the time is well used. When Kadara arrives at the hall, she has considered what must be done to help the Ayelomi even the odds against the well-armored Vulkanar who are burning down their home.

Igiwa and Omi are waiting for her, each a picture of patience. A blanket of leaves is draped over a stand behind them. Kadara embraces and thanks them for returning her to health.

"Are you ready?" Omi holds her hands, looking into her eyes.

"No. No one is ever ready for what we have to do."

"No, no one ever is"—Omi pulls the weave of leaves aside, revealing a new set of armor made for Kadara—"but we can be prepared."

The armor is crafted from what remains of Shaja's leather and additions of petrified wood in various shades of brown, perfect for blending into forest terrain. Protective metals woven into the guards are worked to resemble wet leaves stuck to the leather beneath. The breastplate is a cascade of etchings from Naiwoa, Drakhaal, Teyhala, the Sharu'un, and the Ayelomi, showing Kadara's loyalty to most of Aros and all its people.

She runs her hand along the deep engravings, giving thanks to each nation represented there. There is room, she sees, for a last line of etching. One last kingdom.

Omi notes her hesitation. "Drekan rules his people, Kadara, but no ruler truly speaks for all their subjects. The most loved rulers are the ones who do more listening than speaking. One day, Drekan will be removed from power. Only then can Vulkanar be free to make its own way. Perhaps then they will see the benefit of joining the world the rest of us have been building."

"And if they choose to continue burning it down?"

"Then they will burn with us." Omi embraces Kadara once more and leaves to tend to other matters.

Igiwa nods to Kadara.

"Until then, I have fires to put out. Join me when you can." He calls a wind to carry him like a dragon over the treetops toward the rising smoke.

T is for Tactics, the wisdom of war. Having numbers is nice, but a plan gives you more.

THE AYELOMI HAVE ALWAYS DISAPPEARED INTO THE TREES. Burning the forest down is Drekan's best defense against this. His methods, though, put his people in as much danger as the other combatants on the battlefield. He never runs out of Vulkanar bodies to throw at his problems. He never cares how many Vulkanar bodies won't make it home. Victory is all that matters. Victory at all costs.

He orders the lava to be contained like the energy in his shield and volleyed from beyond the range of the meddlesome tree dragons. These firestones, a fusion of metal and stone wrapped around molten cores, resemble his shield in look and nature. The containers bounce on landing, glowing ever brighter with each impact until exploding with the same destructive force as his shield.

Launching lava, stone, and metal into the trees is effective until it is not. Drekan's shield requires impact to unleash its hidden fury. So, too, do his explosive weapons. Yet, the Ayelomi string nets from the highest points in the canopy. Unseen to the naked eye, the nets allow light and rain and wildlife to travel through as they always have. Drekan's firestones, though, are cradled there, then lowered to the ground. One out of every five makes it through. The rest are sent back. Drekan's forces are decimated. He sends more.

As expected, they withdraw the catapults and attempt a full-scale ground incursion. The Ayelomi are ready. With a mixture of tradition and adaptation, they make new ground. Holes are dug throughout the forest and marked to be filled in when the warring is done. Most will be filled with Vulkanar bodies when that time comes. Until then, a net of leaves is an effective shroud, a pit of spikes an effective weapon.

Other holes are filled from the start with armored Ayelomi warriors waiting for the signal to spring forth and ambush their attackers. The attackers keep coming. They take no ground; they take no blood. Still, they come. Igiwa constructs a wall of everfrost and orders his people to fall back. The Vulkanar soldiers keep coming, undeterred by the unbreakable ice. They are a mindless horde. The people in the armor have ceased to be people; something in them has changed. They have one goal, and Drekan gave it to them.

"He has poisoned their minds," Kadara says to Igiwa as they peer through a spyglass at the northern window in the endless corridor. The throng continues to beat at the ice, some getting too close and freezing there beside the wall, becoming a hazard to the next in line.

"Perhaps," Igiwa says. "Perhaps they are just loyal." He shrugs.

"Loyal enough to give their lives without thought?"

"We all have people for whom we would do the same. What concerns me is that they never attack a single point. Look at them." He waves an arm toward the long wall of ice running west from the river. "They don't *want* to get through."

Kadara peers at the line of warriors charging the wall at random points along its length.

"It's as though a half-hearted order was given—" Igiwa says.

"Before the wall was put up." Kadara finishes for him, her mind running through the advantages Drekan could have gained with this tactic. Her answer comes in the form of a hurried Omi carrying an exhausted messenger bird in one hand and a rolled message in the other.

"It came from the south. Poor little thing must have flown straight here nonstop!" She waves the letter as she jogs, panting as though she too failed to rest on her path of delivery.

"The south? Kala?" Kadara jogs to meet Omi halfway, much to Omi's relief. She takes the small scroll and breaks the seal to reveal the message inside. Her face hardens. "Teyhala sails for Naiwoa. Drekan marches on Castle Osiwo."

"They guard the river." Igiwa points to the intersection of his everfrost wall and the water. Though many Vulkanar knights linger there, none attack the wall; none attempt to enter the forest.

Kadara nods. "I see now. The other soldiers were sent to keep you busy. Drekan fears the Ayelomi will join the battle and flank him."

"Perhaps," Omi says, "but he also fears you, Kadara." She grabs Kadara by the hand and looks at her husband. "Iggy, we need the lake."

He raises an eyebrow at her.

"Our special spot?"

"Sadly, there will be no treaty today, but yes. Our special spot, dear."

Igiwa lifts them on a gentle wind, down through the treetops, and Omi explains. "The Ayelomi never leave our forest, Kadara, but you might." They are set down beside the spout of the Orisunomi Lake, where the waters flow out to become the Apori River. Enormous seedpods float on the surface. "And the fastest way north is via the river." She whispers in Igiwa's ear, and with his wind, he lifts five of the seedpods from the water and sets them on the shore.

Omi gives the first one a swift kick, and the pod cracks open and separates into two halves, the large, spikey seeds spilling out into the water. Kadara helps open the rest. Into six of the makeshift boats, they pile leaves as high as they can and send them down the river one by one. After the six have been sent, Omi turns to Kadara and tells her to get into one. "By now, the seedpods seem commonplace. They may have checked some; they will all have been empty. I will send some down after you to complete the illusion."

Kadara grabs her and hugs her with the intense compression of a field medic's tourniquet. A warm embrace she learned from Omi herself.

"Thank you, Elder-Queen Orisunomi the Fertile."

Omi chuckles at the use of her title and squeezes back.

"I will kick you for that when next we meet." She kisses her cheek and steps back to let her husband say his slow goodbyes.

"Thank you, Elder-King Igiwa the Verdant." Kadara hugs him harder than she should for someone his age.

"Just Jin Igiwa," he says through a stifled cough. "Be safe, Kadara of Aros."

Kadara steps into the pod and, crouching, balances herself in its center before lying on her back. Igiwa blows a full pile of leaves over her and sets the pod onto the water's surface. To the naked eye, Kadara's boat is just another leaf-filled pod floating on the river. Hidden beneath the leaves, the last hope of Aros hears the lovers take flight as she drifts away.

The Apori River is as wide as it is mighty. Collecting water and speed as it travels down through the Grovenkar Hills, it is a beautiful and powerful display of nature. Kadara is jostled by the waves and thinks she may roll but remains hidden beneath her loose shroud of leaves. She can feel the river's speed increase as the springs and tributaries along the way feed it.

As she passes the foot of Canopy Keep, she can feel the pull of her sword and calls it to lie beside her in the bed of shadows. It is of some comfort when the water reaches its highest speeds, and the seedpod is tossed about like feathers before a storm. For hours, the rocks and waves batter her pod, but the leaves and her nerve hold fast. The hills flatten, and the river slows, and Kadara drifts along beneath the shroud of soggy leaves, unwilling to give up her camouflage in favor of knowing where along the river she may be.

After another hour, Kadara can hear muffled voices coming from the shoreline. She strains to listen but cannot make out the words. A small splash sounds near her pod. A moment later, she hears another. The voices rise in argumentative tones. One voice wins out, and within seconds, Kadara understands what has been hitting the water. The fire arrow sinks into the leaves above her. The shoreline voices rise once more in a victorious cry—no doubt they are the forces guarding the river. Kadara pulls in a lungful of air, cuts through the bottom of the pod, and slips out into the current.

And if they choose to continue burning it down?

She swims with the pull of the river for as long as she can before her lungs burn and her vision begins to dim. When it becomes too much, she surfaces among the burnt husks of seedpods drifting toward the Sleeping Mountain. Behind her on the river, the Vulkanar knights continue their fiery target practice on the remaining seedpods, the everfrost wall looming beyond them.

Kadara slips out of the water and rolls onto the shore on the northern side of the eastern turn, the Te-Orani River. She needs to follow this river to reach Naiwoa and join the fight. As she stands, though, she sees that another fight has come to her. She pulls her sword from the water and prepares to defend herself.

U is for Unseen, vanished from sight. In luminous day or tenebrous night.

OF ALL SIX KINGDOMS, VULKANAR WAS INDEED THE MOST CHANGED BY THE ARRIVAL OF THE DRAGONS. What had once been the smallest kingdom became the center of the world with the rise of the Dragon's Grasp and the volcanic fertilization of the surrounding land. This change also provided its people with the stone and metals they would use to make weapons.

In the early days, Vulkanar focused on protecting its land from attackers. The people were farmers and miners, hard-working people who were happy to wake up and to rest each day in the shadow of the Sleeping Mountain.

Over time, factions within the group saw things in differing ways. Soon, Vulkanar was fighting at its borders and within. The Vulkanar Civil War was a long and bloody one.

More Vulkanar rulers died in those decades than in the rest of Aros's history combined. When the survivors emerged, they had perfected the art of killing. They took their armor and weapons and assassins, and they unleashed them on the rest of the world.

While Vulkanar knights are made to take and deliver punishment, their assassins deliver only death. Known as the Unseen, they most often do their work alone, imperceptibly, and with quickness and efficiency.

That Kadara can see two of them in her path does not bode well. These two want to be seen together. Further, they seem to know the path she intends to take. These two want *her* to see them.

But he also fears you, Kadara.

They stand in faded red tunics, belted at the waist. Their skin, naked of any hair, is painted red with the Vulkanar mud. With two swords each, they will be a handful.

Before Kadara can prepare her attack, she is struck from behind. The blow is forceful, knocking her to the ground. She scrambles to her feet, swinging her sword in an arc, but her attacker has vanished.

The two on the road have vanished as well. Kadara spins, searching for the next attack. The blow finds the back of her head. She doubles over in pain, slicing at the empty air and staving off dizziness. The attackers vanish again. Though they are not used to working together, they have the advantage of both numbers and tactics.

She forces her feet to move. A stationary target is far too easy to hit. They follow. Kadara weaves as she runs, cutting the air behind her to hold them off. She can neither see nor hear them, but she can feel their eyes. It feels like the gazes of more than three attackers in pursuit. Searching for an advantage, Kadara realizes she has been to this place before. The rising, jagged juts of rock are all too familiar. She is near the cave that Jabo kept all those years ago. A grunt of pain from behind her interrupts the thought.

She stops hard, digging in her feet, and thrusts in the direction of the sound. Her sword sinks into the chest of one of her pursuers. She becomes visible, gazing into her killer's eyes with tear-filled gratitude.

No ruler truly speaks for all their subjects.

A liberated sigh, a look of sweet release. The weight of the assassin's limp body seems to pull Kadara's soul with it as it slides from her sword. She does not want to kill these people. Have they come here simply to die?

The others do not hesitate. They press the advantage gained by the death of their peer—a trap of flesh, bone, and regrets—at the hedge knight's feet. Kadara slashes in an upward sweep, cutting the attacker approaching from beside her. The attacker smiles and drinks from a flask as he dies.

Kadara releases her sword and dives away as he spits forth a stream of ignited alcohol. She rolls and is back on her feet before the fire breather's body has gone limp. When she looks back, her sword is gone. She snatches one from the deceased assassin.

Kadara may not see or hear the Unseen, but she can feel her sword, wherever it may be. The Unseen press the attack, playing into her hands. She perceives her sword's approach and dodges, cutting it free from the arm holding it. Spinning away, she leaves the Worldsunderer to lie in the red clay.

Another takes up her sword. He drives in hard, and she sidesteps at the last breath. The Worldsunderer sinks into another assassin, and Kadara dances away. As she prepares to dodge again, the assassins change tactics. They attack in threes, and Kadara is forced to parry until an assassin holding the Worldsunderer cuts her borrowed sword into pieces.

He drives the blade of the sword into her abdomen lengthwise, turns in assumed victory, and strolls away. Kadara holds her stomach, staggering as more Unseen reveal themselves around her, celebrating her certain death. She drops to one knee. Another confidently appears. No one could survive a cut that deep.

No one could ever be whole after such a blow.

Kadara smiles and lowers her hands. Whole is what she feels. She holds no blood, no spilled insides, only the World-sunderer. It has never cut her. It never will.

Her sword takes two heads with one strike. She carves through three more before the rest can regroup and disappear from her sight.

She looks at the field of dead around her and shakes her head.

"No more have to die. Not in the name of Drekan. Go home. Let me go on my way."

The assassins answer with a fresh attack. Three metal balls the size of raven's heads bounce toward her. They glow a faint red at first, increasing in intensity with each strike of the ground.

"Or not," she says.

The explosion sends her flying back in pain. She tucks before hitting the ground, landing hard on her hip and rolling as best she can to suffocate the fire. When she stands, her armor is smoldering. She coughs and wipes a trickle of blood from her lip, pulling her sword hard. The assassins count only three now. They hide no more, angrily singing Vulkanar war songs and dancing aside with nimble steps as her sword rushes past from behind them.

They form a staggered triangle, panting and shouting between repetitions of their vocalizing. The magic they've used to shift like rock dragons seems to have waned, become exhausted like its bearers.

As Kadara prepares to attack, a shadow speeds along the landscape toward them. The assassins move with too little urgency. Kadara takes the head of the one closest to her as the dragon dives, screeching with fury. An assassin to her left wakes from his fear-induced trance at the sight of the head rolling past him and slips into the shadows. The third assassin is devoured whole along with a chunk of the sun-baked, red volcanic clay beneath him. Kadara dives clear.

The glorious blue sky dragon's impact sends a cloud of red dust into the air. It roars and slashes at the surrounding ground. The final assassin, still too exhausted to maintain the mask of invisibility, staggers from the shadows and slashes at one of the the dragon's eyes with both swords. The dragon flails in anger and takes to the sky, raining dragonfire down beneath it. Smoke joins the cloud of dust as the assassin unleashes the rest of his explosives in the direction of the beast. As he turns to take cover, Kadara meets him head-on, cutting him in two with his own momentum.

The dragon drops down again and coils around the explosive stones, shielding Kadara from the devastating blast. She keeps her feet but is pushed back so far that the dry, red dust behind her boots makes mounds that rise above her heels. She shuts her eyes tight and drives her sword into the ground, grinding to a halt as the bodies near her continue to tumble like river stones. Looking up, Kadara sees the body of the dragon writhe and contract. It vomits up the dead assassin whole and screeches in misery. It pulls in on itself, shrinking and folding, roaring in pain the whole while.

Kadara leaves her sword in the ground and runs toward it, unaware of why she is drawn to help. The dragon rolls, shifting and convulsing.

Then, it transforms before her eyes.

Kadara is on her knees as she reaches the limp, ragged body before her. His drab robes are stained red with clay and blood. His beard is long and knotted. His eyes are sunken behind closed lids, but Kadara knows they are the kindest eyes in all of Aros. She pulls her mentor close, tears streaming down her face.

"Jabo?"

V is for Vulnerable and exposed. A heart cannot heal if it's constantly closed.

THE WALK IS NOT A LONG ONE, BUT IN KADARA'S STATE, IT IS AN ODYSSEY. She carries Jabo's frail frame, stopping from time to time to let a dizzy spell pass. Their wounds all need to be cleaned and bandaged. She does not know how much internal damage Jabo may have suffered. His breathing is shallow, but it is there. It is hope. And right now, as she's awash in pain and confusion, hope is the perfect light to guide her. She follows it toward the cave she once studied in, hidden near the base of the Sleeping Mountain.

Kadara watches Jabo's weak chest move up and down as she walks. There are lessons, it is clear, that were omitted. The full depth of the connection between her and her mentor, for one. Her sword's pull gets farther and farther away, but she is not concerned. It is an unbreakable connection. Jabo never allowed it in his cave, anyway. Even so, the farther she moves from it, the more the pull fades like a dying torch. Jabo's heartbeat fades too. She quickens her pace.

The weight of night pulls like an anchor on the sun, and it sets at the speed of a sinking boat while Kadara walks. She speaks to Jabo in hushed tones, comforting him when his breathing grows shallow. When she is close to the outcropping, she circles a random set of stones until she thinks she has set her trail there. She apologizes to Jabo for the delay and takes a roundabout path to the hidden cave entrance. When she reaches the false wall, she walks straight through it. Be damned any creature that moved in when Jabo left.

Down the jagged corridor Kadara carries him into the darkness, her memory of the cave serving well enough to guide her. She lays him onto a stone platform, taking care to be gentle, and searches for a lantern. When she finds one, she lights it and searches for another. With two in hand, she places one onto the cold ashes of the fire and lights it to warm the flue.

With the soft, yellow light emanating from the lantern she carries, she searches the cave. She can see it has not changed. She uses this to her advantage, collecting wood and water from the stores, lighting a proper fire, and finding a warm blanket to cloak Jabo in to stop his shivering. Collecting herself can come later. When he is still, she steals away to cover any tracks that lead to the cave opening.

Water is boiled, tea is steeped, and preserves are spooned from dusty jars. By the time Kadara has bandaged their wounds and wrapped her sore ribs, Jabo is awake. With great difficulty and in obvious pain, he pulls himself upright. They sit in silence for some time, sipping tea and eating preserves. Never satisfied with a quiet Jabo, Kadara inches closer and closer until she is sharing the blanket with him. He tries his best not to grin at how ridiculous she can be. Kadara speaks first.

"I'll make a list of people you shouldn't eat."

"Dragons do not read, child."

"Child? My hair is as gray as yours."

"Grayer."

Kadara rises and prepares more tea. She takes the blanket with her.

Jabo smiles and shakes his head. "You can say you are angry."

It's Kadara's turn to shake her head.

"I wouldn't know what to be angry *about*, Jabo. You never lied to me; you never misled me. Everything you ever told me was true. You just left out some very important details. You gave me the Ileri stone, though. It led me back here. I suppose it led me to the answers, if you are willing to share them."

Jabo hangs his head at the mention of the Ileri stone. Kadara sits beside him again, wrapping a portion of the blanket around his small shoulders and touching the back of his hand.

"Do you remember the Teyhalan practice of sharing stories?"

Jabo nods, a tear forming in his eye.

"I'll go first."

Kadara recounts to Jabo her journey since the day the Ileri stone awoke. She is well-practiced at sharing her story, and Jabo is delighted and saddened and humored at all the appropriate places. His eyes soften when she speaks of Greyhaal, as if remembering an old friend. The hint of a smirk passes over his lips when he hears of Isaleti. A grave look of contemplation, spread across his face by the mention of Sunni Ojiji, is abandoned for shock at the recounting of how the amulet was shattered, and his expression shifts to outright joy while Kadara speaks of Jin Igiwa.

When she finishes sharing her tale, Kadara rises to make more tea, feeling the weight of Jabo's story even before its telling.

As she pours the water, she hears the hollow, crackling sound of crystalline ice forming behind her. When she turns,

Jabo holds in his shaking palm a small statue of a dragon made from everfrost.

"Its permanence is a lie," he says. He floats the figurine on a minor wind to settle it in the fire. There it sits, like glass, unmoving and unbothered by heat or time. "Everything is impermanent, but nothing is more so than magic. We were never meant to linger here."

Kadara hands him a cup of tea, and he thanks her with his eyes while sipping.

"Wizards are often clever, always kind." He places the cup down. "The sight of one frenzies a dragon more than any glorious battle. There are no schools of wizardry, no wizarding lineage. The birth of a wizard is as random as the color of a dragon."

"None have been witnessed as children, and most are far too reclusive to offer any personal history," Kadara says, elbowing Jabo.

He smiles and nods.

"Wizards are exceptionally rare. A wizard who lives long is far rarer." He pauses, taking a long draw of his tea while collecting his thoughts. "When a dragon is overcome by its desire to do good, it transforms, for a time, into a wizard. It can be a confusing time. Many forget what they once were. Some, like Lilo Kuta, never know of our true nature. They sacrifice themselves before the truth can be revealed to them.

We all have the same intention, the same purpose as the dragons once had—to stop the fighting. To bring peace to Aros." He studies her face.

Kadara watches the everfrost dragon in the fire. The orange and yellow reflections dancing over its surface make it look like it's moving.

"How long have you known?" She faces him, taking in words from his face that he does not say out loud. *I love you, and I am sorry, and there is more.*

"I've known since long before the day I gave Ologun the dragonstone shard he used to make your sword." *I love you, and I am sorry, and there is more.* "This world is not right, Kadara. When the dragons were spat forth from the crust of Aros, it was to quell the fighting and return to Aros to be one with her again. All these years . . ." His voice trails off, and he raises his empty teacup to his lips and places it back down again. "The fighting, the bloodshed, the madness. Hundreds of years of it. It changed the dragons. It drove us insane. When we turned to Inati N'tan for guidance, he returned to the Sleeping Mountain, sealing the way behind him, abandoning and deserting us here. The madness . . ."

Jabo rises to refill the cups, and Kadara helps him stand. When he returns, his arms are shaking. Kadara takes the cups and steadies his hands.

"You need to rest," she says.

"I need to finish." Jabo rubs his hands and looks into her eyes. *I love you, and I am sorry, and there is more.* "I cannot become that *thing* again, Kadara. The longer we live, the larger the dragon gets. Stronger, angrier, always thrashing about. Always trying to get loose."

He sits and takes the warm cup from Kadara. Sipping the tea seems to calm him some. "It should be done by now. All the fighting should have ended. We try so hard for peace—but the madness. It seems to be driven by the very magic meant to stop it . . ." He trails off again and sips his tea. "I told Ologun to make that sword, Kadara, and when I was certain you would use it only for good, I gave you my Ileri stone and made you forget. It guided you on quite a journey, yes, but it was meant only to guide you to me, and only when I lost control.

"As a wizard, I can do so much good but only for so long. Over time, the dragon wins, or the wizard dies. I would rather die as a wizard. If I must die a dragon, let it be quick and let it be by your hand." A tear rolls down his aged cheek, leaving a shining trail from his golden eye to the tip of his trembling chin. "This was a horrible thing to put on you, Kadara. It is an even more horrible thing I am asking of you, but I must. Now, while we can. Pull the dragonstone from my blood and strike me down for the good of all Aros."

"I love you, and I forgive you, and that is all," Kadara says. She wraps her arms around him and holds him until he is holding her back, and they are warm and safe and comforted by each other's presence, as two reacquainted loved ones so often are.

"Kadara."

"You old fool." Kadara stands. "Did you hear none of the story I shared? After we fought, you carried me to where I would be near no battles while you rampaged across Aros." She takes him by the hand and makes him stand with her. "Only days ago, though a battle raged near here, you appeared over the fertile plains when I needed you most and attacked my enemies. Only then did you turn into a wizard again."

The heaviness in Jabo's brow lightens.

"Perhaps not out of desire to do good," Kadara says, "but in response to having done so."

"Dragons can do good," Jabo says, his eyes now alight with hope.

"'Slay a thing for what it does, not for what it is.' Besides, I can't feel the dragonstone in your blood when you are in wizard form. I never could." Kadara stops, her smile collapsing like a windblown tent.

"What is it?"

"When the orchard falls silent, the storm is never far behind. My sword. It's moving toward us."

W is for Waiting, through patience and will. Time tends to move fast when your mind has been stilled.

KADARA RESISTS THE URGE TO CALL HER SWORD TO HER SIDE, OPTING INSTEAD FOR THE ADVANTAGE OF KNOWING WHERE HER ENEMIES ARE. Whoever has her sword is following her trail from the site of the dragon attack. They waded through a sea of dead to take her sword and followed the deep-set footprints of one whom they must have believed to be the only survivor, as Kadara had carried Orun Jabo the entire way. The speed of their travel suggests their tracking is done from horseback.

These are plains knights. They are Vulkanar.

Kadara looks around. This place has been here for countless years but has never been discovered. It has never been searched for, either. The long corridor masks the light from within but only so well. If the Vulkanar knights seek a fire, if they seek a hidden shelter, they will find it. Jabo's fragile frame is not fit for battle. She knows this. His injuries have not yet healed. The everfrost dragon watches her from within the fire, unbothered by its circumstances.

The sword draws nearer. Any defensive measures Kadara might take would alert the hunters, making Jabo and her trapped targets. The outcropping is among others, but it's too far out in the open to risk sprinting from it. Their pursuers would see them and, with horses, run them down in no time.

Kadara looks at Jabo. He is calm. He is waiting.

"Does your cheese come directly from the goat?"

He is right. She sits beside him and watches the fire dance. Change will come; they need not worry that it hasn't yet. Patience.

It is not long before they hear the thunder of hooves rolling across the Vulkanar clay. An entire battalion, from the sound of it. They follow her path, circling the fingers of black rock jutting from the ground just as she had. The trail ends there. Kadara chides herself for not leading the trail away after securing Jabo. She knows, though, that it would only have gained them time; already, horses are sweeping in wider arcs while others can be heard creating a perimeter.

Her sword slows its approach. She can feel it calling to her as it is carried to within the perimeter of hoof falls in the distance.

An explosion rocks the cave and surrounding area, sending gravel and sand down on the two old friends as they sit and wait. Another goes off in the distance. The Vulkanar are probing, hoping to expose the cave or cause enough panic to make the hidden expose themselves.

It will not work. Patience is an ethereal armor, fortified by calmness, stillness.

The day dims as the two old friends wait and listen to the clanking sound of tent poles being hammered into the surrounding ground. The enemy has patience as well. When four stakes have been set, Kadara senses her sword moving toward the sound. The first tent goes to the one who carries the Worldsunderer. These soldiers have a leader. More tents are raised, and the horses are gathered to stomp and neigh in one place. Kadara longs for the expanse of hearing she enjoyed in the amulet's light as she mentally constructs an image of the scene around the hidden cave.

Though Jabo can surely sense her thoughts, he does not speak to quell them and risk being heard by the hunters so near to them. When the hammering stops, and it seems all the tents have been raised, the sword moves toward where the remaining sounds are clustered. The din of voices quiets.

Kadara feels the sword being lifted. Voices rise in unison. The sword is lowered. The voices fall. Their leader wishes to speak.

"I know you're here somewhere." The voice of Drekan echoes through the landscape. "Unsworn. The knight from the forest. I found your wretched sword."

Kadara feels it get tossed to the ground.

"I followed your panicked footsteps from where you escaped my assassins. I bring you death, trespasser."

The voices rise again, cheering for the impending slaughter. When they fall, he continues. "Of course, that death need not be yours. Not if you give me what I want. Not if you tell us how to find the blue dragon. I know Jabo protects it."

An explosion shakes the cave.

"I know it is him you ran to. The hovel he slinks away to is here somewhere."

Another explosion blows through the rock formations farther away.

"I only need him to find the dragon. Spare me the time it will take to find you, and I will spare your life. Make me find you, and you will wish you'd died burning in the forest."

The voices rise again. Kadara looks at Jabo. He yawns. Patience.

The night brings the promised encampment, and as soon as the morning light allows, the soldiers return to destroying the area surrounding Jabo's home in the name of finding the enemy. Kadara and Jabo sit and sip tea, covering their cups whenever a blast disturbs the cave enough to send sand and rubble down onto them. When night falls, Drekan tries again.

"Give me the wizard, knight, or I will bring the Sleeping Mountain down on your head." The Vulkanar soldiers cheer at the notion. "We will not stop until we find you. These men answer to an endless master. We will not stop."

Jabo chews his jerky and watches the fire. The everfrost dragon sits waiting, unbothered. Jabo sighs and smiles at the dragon. Kadara rises to make more tea, but Jabo stops her and makes it himself. He points at the dragon and at her and smiles. Kadara understands. Patience.

In the morning, the explosions double in frequency. Jabo grins at each one, knowing that they represent Drekan's frustration. Kadara knows, though, that Drekan has patience on his side as well. There are only so many rocks to destroy before you find the right one.

This time, night falls on an angry Vulkanar king. He picks up the sword and flings it into the air. It clatters against the rocks Kadara and Jabo hide within. They listen to his roaring screams of frustration before more explosions drown them out.

The cave is rocked like a seedpod on a raging river. Kadara sees a crack form in the stone ceiling. It starts above the tea stand and moves away from her to the area over Jabo's head, dislodging a boulder. Kadara grabs Jabo by the shoulders and pulls hard, moving him in time for the boulder to slam down behind him. Before it does, she hears her sword clatter against the wall of the cave outside. Kadara had pulled with too much of herself—all of herself—and the effort pulled her sword as well. She saved Jabo but gave away their position.

Patience has served them well until now. Action will need to take the reins.

"Alas." The mocking voice is Drekan's, but only in part. It swirls with another, older, deeper voice. The two fight for dominance in his mad cry. "Did you think you could elude me forever?"

Jabo's breath catches. For the first time since Kadara met him, he seems afraid.

"Inati N'tan," Jabo says and turns to Kadara with fear in his tear-filled eyes. *I love you, and I am sorry, and there is more.*

Drekan gives them no time. The rock above them explodes into a thousand jagged fragments. Before Kadara can react, Jabo bursts into dragon form, his head immense and expanding faster than uncorked dreams. His enormous, teary eyes change color as the dragon's amber and Jabo's gold mottle together to gleam like bronzed clouds.

He continues to grow as Kadara screams in fear and sadness. His mouth, the size of the room and growing, swallows her whole. Kadara falls and falls for what feels like forever through a sideways and endless corridor. When she thinks she will go mad from falling, she blinks and is standing in the now cozy cave room alone.

X is for Xenolith, stone within stone. What essence remains when we're no more than bones?

KADARA SITS ALONE AND WEEPING AT THE CENTER OF THE LABYRINTH SHE ONCE CALLED ORUN JABO. His voice echoes from the surrounding walls.

"Only a wizard can craft a labyrinth, and only once," it says. "What is the purpose of a labyrinth, Kadara?"

She shakes her head, looking at the space around her.

"I don't know anymore, Jabo."

"What is at the end of this labyrinth, Kadara?"

The echoes of Jabo's voice fade, and Kadara takes wood to the waning fire. Inside, the tiny dragon sits watching her. It wavers and blurs behind the thin film of tears coating her eyes. Kadara blinks them away and tosses in the log.

Outside, the explosions have subsided. Drekan has a location. It will not be long until he sends his troops in to drag her out and demand to know the whereabouts of the wizard. They will leave empty-handed.

Kadara looks toward what was once the long corridor to the cave entrance. The walls appear older and paler than before. She rubs her hand along the wall nearest to her. It reminds her of the Greyhaal labyrinth, and she sheds a silent tear for Lilo Kuta. To never have known her true nature was probably a blessing.

Everywhere she looks, she sees Jabo, hears his voice, smells his robes and pipe. It is an abrasive emotion, like sand on raw skin, but she never wants to leave. They would drag her out if they could, but they cannot.

"A labyrinth prevents certain people from passing through." Kadara laughs through her tears. "And I am at the center." The old fool has saved her again. Drekan and his men may enter, but they will never reach her as long as she is patient.

They try anyway, for days. Hundreds upon hundreds of them enter in pairs and singles and groups, and all fail. Kadara is close enough to touch them, but they cannot see her; they see only endless halls and doorways to more. They enter as a horde and exit in staggered, confused groups.

Drekan screams in fury, calling out in his layered voice.

"Bring her to me," Kadara hears him scream. "Bring me her body so I can watch it burn."

Before long, she is listening to him execute soldiers who return empty-handed. "You can save these men," he screams. "You can save them all by showing yourself."

She waits.

When they cannot unravel the path to Kadara, they resort to destroying walls, smashing and blowing open alternative paths that lead to nowhere. Jabo was an ancient dragon. His labyrinth is enormous. All that Kadara can do is wait and watch. She can see the exit but dares not walk into the hands of Drekan.

She calls her sword, pulls at it, but its magic cannot penetrate the labyrinth.

After a week, Drekan grows tired of waiting. He tries one last plea. "There is nothing good about a wizard, Dragonslayer, nothing . . . natural. Their very existence threatens all of Aros. Aid me in my task. Help me rid our land of this blight. Help me save the world. Is that not what you want? Is it not what all of us want?"

He pauses, as if believing she will reconsider and emerge. When she does not, his mask of calm slips away. "Fine. I would prefer your head beside Orun Jabo's, but I am happy to place his upon two stakes when I am through with him. A pity you won't be there to see it."

His rage renewed, he calls out to his men in his layered voice and orders a full assault on the surrounding area. "If you will not emerge when called, you will not emerge at all."

The cave shakes for so long that Kadara thinks of the promised rise of Sunni Ojiji. She watches as the rocks above and beyond the exit crumble and slide, blocking the way out behind a barricade of stone and grit.

Sleep trades places with eating preserves and drinking tea and talking to the walls of Jabo's echoing voice for days. Kadara's grief becomes a new labyrinth within the larger one, leading her down endless corridors of despair. She wills herself to become lost in it, dousing the lamps of hope and happiness along the way.

She is trapped, but she is here, with Jabo. She can think of worse places to be buried. Some graves are made of ashes; others are under the sea. Some people never get buried at all. Still, there are promises to keep. Without her sword, keeping them will be difficult. She paces the room, wishing for a way to get a message to her friends, to let them know she is here.

The thought falls away like desert sands, replaced by concern. Drekan attacked Naiwoa to find her and draw out Jabo. He could go after Jin Igiwa next, or Isaleti. And using the voice of Inati N'tan, no less.

Kadara presses her hand against the wall and speaks to her mentor.

"This world just takes and takes." She presses her other hand to the wall and closes her eyes. "And sometimes it gives things it never should." She focuses, her head lowered, sweat forming on her brow. The cavern shakes with a small, concentrated tremor, and Kadara presses harder. "Someone needs to make it right." Her breathing becomes ragged, and her legs become weak with pain, but she persists. She cannot call her sword, but she can call the shard.

With a final, jerking, half-call, half-pull, she flies backward onto the ground, her hands clasped together. She ignores the pain as she sits up and opens her palms, peering into them. Within, she holds Jabo's last gift. A small, sunrise-colored stone gleams in the dark cavern of her grasp. She laughs until her ribs are sore and stands, rubbing the stone's smooth surface. She can feel its presence just as she can feel her sword.

When she sleeps that night, she sleeps holding the stone. In her dreams, she follows the stone to Jabo, and he waits like an everfrost dragon in a sea of fire.

She thinks of the stone first when she wakes in the morning. With it in her hand, the pull of her sword is far stronger. Try as she might, however, she still cannot call it through the labyrinthine magic.

The stone, though, she controls with ease. She passes the time tossing and pulling the stone. She flings it down one of the many corridors leading from the cozy cave room and pulls it back to catch it. Soon, she takes to calling the stone instead. She throws it and calls it back with ease.

Over time, she finds that if she leaves it somewhere at night, she will wake with it in her hand. She gets more and more daring with her new prize, throwing it as far down the unlit corridors as she can and leaving it until it reappears. One night, she tosses it and curls up by the fire like a tired desert lion. When she wakes, she is in the corridor and shivering, the gem in her hand.

She tosses the stone aside, blaming a lack of tea, and finds her way back to the cozy bed by the fire. As she drifts off to sleep, she feels the pull of the stone. She ignores it and rolls over. The ground is warm one moment and cold the next. She opens her eyes and finds she is back in the corridor, with the stone in her hand. Clutching it, she returns to bed.

In the morning, she places the stone down and crosses the room. She sits by the fire and stares at the stone, feeling its pull and resisting the urge to pull back. Such a simple little thing it is: not quite round, with a smooth, flat side that is perfect for resting it on. Much like her sword was cast to fit in her hand, the stone seems destined to be held by her. To her, it is Jabo and peace and wholeness. It is part of her and part of him and all that she has left of him, save for this maze of loneliness and the everfrost dragon that stares at her from within the fire.

She closes her eyes as a swell of emotion fills her. When she opens them, she is sitting with the stone in her fist, across the room from the fire. She gasps for air, as if coming up from the darkened depths of misunderstanding, to breathe in new light, new truths. In no time, the stone is back in place, and Kadara is again beside the fire.

She stares at the stone, waiting. She thinks of Jabo, of her friends, of her home. Nothing happens. She thinks of her sword and the feeling of reunion that floods her when it is in her palm. Still, nothing changes. She waits and waits and, before long, falls asleep to wake up in the place of the stone, holding it in her hand. Back to her bed beside the fire she takes the stone and sleeps until what must surely be morning.

Y is for Yearning, a hole in your heart. The grief never ends, but the healing must start.

KADARA WAKES FROM A DREAM THAT SHE IS ESCAPING FROM DROWNING, HAVING FOUND THE SURFACE AND BREACHED IT FOR AN INSTANT. She rubs the shiny orange stone and turns it over in her hand, considering its magic. In her mind ring the words of Orisunomi.

"A wizard can only create an Ileri stone once in their life."

"And in their death?" Kadara tosses the stone into the fire and yanks it back, concerned that it might pull her in instead.

And in his death?

She squeezes the stone, both to hide it from her view and to prevent it from ever leaving her possession. As it is with her blood, the dragonstone is intertwined with Jabo's essence. From the day they first fought before an audience of

Ologun's menagerie, they have been on a path to becoming one.

What Kadara pulled from the labyrinth walls is not only dragonstone but the pieces of Jabo that had bonded with it over time. Pieces that she could never lose because they are part of something more. They are a part of the Worldsunderer. They are a part of her. She could never have left this place without them.

Outside the cave, soldiers knock down the tents and drag them away. They take her sword with them. She does not try to stop them, doesn't pull at her sword to keep it near. They think she is dead. Kadara prefers it that way.

She feels her sword grow farther and farther away until she cannot feel it anymore and feels, instead, a deeper hole inside her than before. Her food and fresh water supplies dwindling, she waits with patience, knowing change will come, while learning to understand her stone.

Within days, she can call herself to the stone at will, instead of the other way around. She sets it beside the fire and crosses the room. Her eyes are set, focused not on the strange stone but on the part of her that is missing it. As she stops existing there and begins existing beside the fire, stone in hand, she gains a sense of calm. She does not feel fulfilled, though, as if there is still more to the meal and she has saved some room.

True hunger sets in, vying with the sense of lack to see which can make her feel emptier. Having survived thus far on jarred fruits and water, her body has been contracting for some time now, the skin tightening over her cheekbones and ribs. Kadara finds solace in the thought that her last days will be spent in the shell of Jabo while holding a part of him in her hand.

She tosses the stone across the room and joins it before it can fall to the cave floor. Back toward the fire she tosses it, joining it again while it's still in midair. She chuckles, dizzy from the stone-calling and the lack of sustenance. She half-sits, half-collapses onto her bed beside the fire, staring at the stone. It pulls at her, even there in her hand, and she complies in half-delirium. She feels herself shift and go nowhere. She feels the stone do the same. The thought occurs that she might make herself more whole.

Focusing on the hole in her heart, she thinks of filling it with the stone, with Jabo's love, with the little emotion she is still strong enough to express. She senses the stone shift. It shimmers and disappears from her trembling hand, replaced by fallen tears. In turn, the saddened sigh she exhales is replaced by sudden screaming. She falls onto the floor, clutching her chest and gasping for air in between her screeches of pain.

A fire burns deep within her veins, boiling her from the inside.

Her blood is like tiny knives tumbling against the walls of her arteries. The pain tears outward from her chest, each heartbeat shooting arrows of dragonfire through her circulatory system. Her brown eyes feel as though they may be pressed from her skull, and golden, fractured lines form outward from the pupils. She rolls over, pushing herself onto her hands and knees, and vomits a beast-like roar of agony. It lasts for so long that she passes out from the lack of oxygen.

Kadara wakes gasping and clutching for the stone. The pain has faded like childhood memories. She looks around, searching for the stone but knowing well the space it occupies. It is inside her; it is *of* her. She has become a part of the larger whole, like a throne made of stones, a sword-treaded wheel. She senses, again, her sword. The pull is powerful, as though it sits beside her, despite the vast distance between them.

Pieces of her Ayelomi-crafted armor dot the ruins of the labyrinth. Kadara collects them and puts them on with reverence, remembering the day she first donned armor in the amulet's light. A pang of hunger rolls through her belly like a lost storm, and she thinks hard of a reunion with her sword. She calls it, pulling, pleading with it to overcome a magic she knows cannot be bypassed.

Harder and harder she pulls and calls, the strain making her eyes roll, her chest heave. Kadara reaches out with the whole of her, her arms shaking, thrust toward the direction of her sword. She reaches out with the unknown parts of her, the new parts made of dragonstone and dragon blood and Jabo. She pulls and calls and, at last, detects an answer. It is deep within her. She closes her eyes and lets the answer ring free.

She cannot call the sword, but the sword can call her.

She opens her eyes onto a world of water, of darkness below and light above, her sword in hand. Kicking hard, Kadara reaches the surface and sucks in fresh air. The light of the sun blinds her, and she squints against it before splashing and kicking for what looks like a shore. When she reaches it, she coughs up the murky water she swallowed in her struggles. It splashes onto bloodstained mud.

Kadara looks up, and in the distance, she sees smoke rising from the ridge of Castle Osiwo. Behind her, beyond the stretch of lake she pulled herself from, she sees Forgehold, the stronghold of Vulkanar, jutting from the northern base of the Sleeping Mountain.

Drekan saw fit to have her sword tossed into the center of Osiwo Lake, the deep, pooling deposit of the Te-Orani River, which empties into the floodplains. Kadara stands like a flower unfolding, taking in the devastation that has befallen the once-proud kingdom: burnt homes, broken fortifications, and smoldering wreckage. She stumbles east into the chaos, the faces of Senari and Rodahn flashing in her mind with every blink of her eyes.

Z is for Zenith, the apex, the crown. You cut off the head, and the rest will fall down.

IT IS NOT A SIMPLE THING TO DESTROY RIVER PEOPLE WITH FIRE. Kadara wades through bogs and guilt alike as she searches the region for any sign that the flame of the Naiwoan people still burns. With each step, she renews the ungrantable wish that she had made it here in time. The river dragons, often seen sunning on the shore, are hiding in their underwater dens to avoid the smoke, the burning, the chaos. There is no glory to be seen here. This is not battle; this is slaughter.

She travels on foot and by calling herself to her sword, crossing canals of muddied water and pulling the bodies of innocent Naiwoans to dry shores as she goes.

Kadara hones her new skill as she journeys, throwing the Worldsunderer ahead of her and joining it there before it touches the ground. Her blood rushes with each call, and the exhilaration energizes her. It mixes like freshwater and the sea at the mouth of the delta, swirling with the bile that forms each time an unarmed body is found floating along her path.

Before long, she is traveling with reckless abandon. She pulls too hard to the left with one errant throw and lands in the burning husk of a torched tree.

Kadara thinks of screaming only after she extracts herself unharmed, save for some bruises and scorched armor. She holds her hand over the fire, watching the flames lick at her skin without effect. It makes her uneasy, and she pulls her hand back and rubs it. How much of her has changed?

Careful to avoid deep holes where dragons may sleep, Kadara continues to scout the area. In the distance, she sees a column of smoke that rises slowly, without fury: smoke from a campfire. The smoke will lead to soldiers, to food. She moves like a stalking lion, crouched low against the dried, burnt grass. When she is close, she crawls along the ground to keep cover, watching and listening.

Vulkanar soldiers patrol the camp. In the open shell of their lazy perimeter, Kadara sees the pearl of a prisoner cage. It is full of fisherfolk and ferry people, not fighters. It is full of people waiting to be freed. They, like her empty stomach, will have to wait a while more. The sun is too high for ambush, and she cannot risk having a Vulkanar soldier escape and alert others. She rolls onto her back and watches the clouds overhead mix with the rising smoke. When she thinks sleep will come, it evades her, adrenaline and hunger each pinning an eye open. Night falls, and Kadara rises.

The Vulkanar soldiers sing songs of old and honorable wars while they lay waste to a precious land within eyesight of its once-respected stronghold. Roast beast turns on spits over their enormous campfire, dripping grease onto the embers below it. The prisoners watch from behind the bars, no doubt starving. The sudden appearance of a sword in the cook's chest interrupts the singing.

"Too far to the left."

Kadara smiles from the shadows, having expected the sword to land in the beast instead. Before the closest soldier can rise, Kadara is beside the cook, finishing the killing stroke with a flourish and a toothy grin.

She spins, sending the sword into the vines holding the cage together. Meeting her sword there, she yells for the prisoners to run before turning back to the stunned soldiers. With her eyes wild, draped in armor honoring all but them, Kadara addresses the Vulkanar.

"You are trespassing on Naiwoan royal land," she says. "Leave at once by order of Queen Senari of the Riverborn." She slashes through the rest of the cage wall. "Or hope I will show you mercy."

The most heavily armored of the soldiers steps forward.

"No one hopes in Vulkanar."

Kadara has been far too long without her sword. She is a dragon who has found her tail. It is her balance, her weapon, her tool.

Her eyes, like two Vulkanar shields, beam with golden cracks that flash with lightning every time she blinks.

The prisoners run north, glancing back as often as they dare, fearing both the soldiers and their savior.

With each glance, they count fewer Vulkanar. Their savior appears and disappears at will, taking lives like Death itself.

When only the soldier who spoke of hope remains, Kadara cuts away his armor while he grimaces. Her eyes are raging fires as she raises his chin with her knee, forcing him to look at her.

"You are permitted hope here," she says to him, "for this is Naiwoa."

The Vulkanar soldier laughs a frigid, empty laugh.

"Call it what you will, wizard. It belongs to Drekan now. All will belong to Drekan."

"I have seen the soil your words are rooted in. Your tongue bears tainted fruit."

"He is far more than a man." The soldier speaks faster now, as if his last words risk being lost. "Far more even than you, and he will burn the whole of Aros to destroy you and your kind—"

Kadara removes his head in a forceful strike, and his limp body folds away. His last words dissipate like the ether of dreams.

"My kind? Judge the fruit by how it nourishes, not by how it looks on the branch." What is she becoming? A wizard she is not. All wizards are good. She is angry.

She approaches the fire, cuts flesh from the dripping roast, and devours it before roaring a yell of anger that frightens even her. When she turns back, the last of the prisoners have disappeared into the wetlands. She looks west toward Vulkanar land and begins walking.

The days roll into nights as Kadara wanders. She cuts through the floodplains in silence, growing more adept at calling herself to her sword and freeing more prisoners along the way. They come to call her the Ghost of Naiwoa.

Kadara welcomes the legend. It will sow fear and confusion in Drekan's ranks. When she encounters a long line of soldiers all heading west, she stills her sword and follows at a safe distance. They lead her to a much larger encampment on the edge of Naiwoan land. She perches in the shadows on a nearby ridge, overlooking the mass of soldiers, horses, siege engines, and assassins.

Drekan prepared for war while the rest of the world sowed peace. He has not prepared for Kadara's reaping.

Ash drifts across the ruined plains like falling snow. Kadara presses a hand to her chest, half-expecting to feel the comforting warmth of her shattered amulet. Instead, she feels only the pulse of her own heartbeat, heavy with regret. In the distance, a drumbeat of thunder rumbles, echoing the rage stirring in her blood.

She can sense it now, the dragon-soul within her, inherited from Jabo's last gift. Another dormant inheritance, overripe with destiny. "Ghost, wizard, dragonslayer. I'll be whatever it takes to stop you."

She tosses her sword into the night and calls herself into the darkness. Somewhere far away, a rumble rises from deep beneath the desert sands, as though the world itself is calling her name.

Thank you to the wonderful team of beta readers who took the time to live in Aros for a short while as it was being constructed. I do so hope the noise wasn't too bothersome.

Special thanks to Cha, Rob, and Sarah, who did the heavy lifting of identifying, and forcing me to acknowledge, the shortcomings in a story greatly influenced by them well in advance of it being written.

Thank you to my editor, Heather, who understands that each word is its own song. And helped me hit all the right notes.

A thank you as well to all of the writers who came before me and filled my dreams with dragons. To carry on the tradition is an honor.

R.E. Lockett is a husband, father of two, and avid reader with a background in Literature. He's an illustrator, songwriter, and singer whose love of storytelling has produced five children's books celebrating nature and friendship: The Race to Flutter Flower Field, Monet and the Monster Magic, Bear Bridge, Griz and Oz, and There Used to Be a Forest Here. His narrative poetry collection, Thin Windows, blends fantasy, sci-fi, and horror through surreal, lyrical verse.

www.ingramcontent.com/pod-product-compliance
Lightning Source LLC
LaVergne TN
LVHW032007070526
838202LV00059B/6340